Suitcases

A Clock or a Crown?

By Caroline Logue

Illustrated by Sarah Bowie

SUITCASES: A CLOCK OR A CROWN?

First published in 2015 by
Little Island Books
7 Kenilworth Park
Dublin 6W
Ireland

ISBN: 978-1910411-29-2

A British Library Cataloguing in Publication record for this book is available from the British Library.

Cover image by Sarah Bowie; designed by Martin Reilly.

Printed in Poland by Drukarnia Skleniarz.

Typeset by Martin Reilly in Merriweather (by Ebin Sorkin) and Elsie Swash Caps (by Alejandro Inler).

Little Island receives financial assistance from the Arts Council / An Chomhairle Ealaíon and from the Arts Council of Northern Ireland.

10 9 8 7 6 5 4 3 2 1

Contents

For Carolines and Johns,
Emilys and Matthews,

and the rebel-yell
children in all of us.

Acknowledgements

Many people helped to get *A Clock or a Crown?* into print, most particularly Siobhán Parkinson, publisher and editor at Little Island. Thanks also to Gráinne Clear of Little Island and Yasmin O'Grady of A Country House Writers' Weekend. Thanks beyond thanks to all my friends for their unswerving encouragement, especially Colleen and Ros. And eternal gratitude to my maternal grandmother, Caroline Logue, who died when I was six. By all accounts she was an amazing teacher, so I really hope she would have approved of this book and been proud that I borrowed her name for it.

About the Author

Caroline Logue lives in Dublin and has a secret life as a journalist and travel writer. She also writes short stories, poems and radio plays, but this is her first proper bit of writing (because it's for kids!). When she needs an extra lick of inspiration she asks her tiny dog, Roly, as she seriously believes he's magic.

The Very Beginning

As Jenny skipped into the wide hallway of the solid old farmhouse, her left hand began to tingle. It was as if it could already feel the doorknob heat off the Best Bedroom of All – the place where beginnings began.

They had arrived with a rasp of car brakes and a scrunch of garden gravel, followed by Mum and Dad's soft voices being glad those windy lanes were behind them.

Aunty Jasmine had appeared straight away, framed in the double doorway, her toasty-brown skin making her teeth look even whiter. Her welcoming smile for Jenny was wide and her arms were wider still. She hugged her beloved niece.

Uncle Donal was so tall that Jenny had to crick her neck to look at him. But he quickly crouched to embrace her, making his thin legs superhero-bendy, like in cartoons.

As the four adults did smacky mwah-kisses on each other's cheeks and their conversation buzzed like bees, Jenny stood apart and breathed deeply to quell the tingling that had spread from her fingers to every-where else. A question mark was forming in her mind:

Where
in the
world
would
the
magic
take
her
this

time?

But Jenny didn't dare gaze up the stairs towards the Best Bedroom of All. She always left That One for last. Other places had to come first, before the special adventures could begin.

Each time Jenny arrived at Aunty Jasmine and Uncle Donal's country house, she greeted her least favourite creature – toothy old Mrs Croc – with two stubby kicks. So that's what she did this time too. Duff! Duff!

A great-great-great explorer uncle of Aunty Jasmine's had wrestled Mrs Crocodile to the ground in the steamy jungles of Africa years and years ago.

These days the front half of Mrs Croc's scaly body squatted silently in the hall outside the dining-room door, her savage teeth bared in a permanent snarl.

Owww, yelped Jenny (but only in her head, so as not to startle Mum) after her sharp kicks to Mrs C. She hopped from foot to foot in front of the empty fireplace until her burning toes cooled. *I won't do that so hard again!*

If the black snoozy cat wasn't on the massive red rug, and no-one was there to tell you to stop, you could do a long whooshy slide towards the bottom of the stairs. If you did it hard enough, you could get the whole way. And, luckily for Jenny, the black snoozy cat had just wandered off the rug.

Jenny glanced at Mum and Dad and Uncle Donal and Aunty Jasmine. They were wired deep into fast circles of conversation and taking no notice of her at all.

Whoooooooo-sssss-*hhhhhh!*

As soon as she'd hopped from the scrunched-up rug to the first stair, Jenny turned to wave and catch her dad's eye.

'Upstairs.' She pointed and mouthed at the same time.

Her father's eyes crinkled in an encouraging grin. He gave her a high thumbs-up and then patted down his spiky fair hair.

'See you later, Dad.'

In no time at all Jenny had reached Mr Leopard, who lay spreadeagled at the wide turn half-way up the staircase.

Mr Leopard had had his sleek spotty coat sliced off by Aunty Jasmine's

bloodthirsty several-greats uncle, which Jenny often thought must have been really painful. Still, at least he didn't hurt now, even when Aunty Jasmine and Uncle Donal and their friends and relations walked all over him. Years of feet had flattened Mr Leopard into a proper rug, although his ears still popped up, and the end of his raggedy tail, after the Sellotaped part, was oddly fat.

At the top of the staircase a landing with wooden railings went all the way around inside. Jenny wanted to say the highest part of the ceiling there was a rectangle shape, but it had curves at each corner so she knew that wasn't quite right.

'When you're older and wiser, you'll know a lot more words,' Mum often said, as she helped Jenny find ones to match her thoughts. 'Especially if you keep reading all those books you love so much.'

If you lifted your eyes to the place that was softer than a rectangle and then tilted your head, you could see the sky sideways through a joined-up necklace of windows.

Jenny was on the top stair now. Where It Happens was getting closer.

When she reached the wooden landing, Jenny always turned left.

The Middle Beginning

The tingling had been replaced by fluttery yawns and wake-up stretches in Jenny's stomach.

Not tooo sooon. When her Sensible Self spoke in Jenny's head she was hooty, like an owl. But soothing too, the way Mum sometimes spoke when Jenny felt sick or couldn't sleep. *Visit the other bedroooms first. It might not haaappen this time. Not tooo sooon.*

Take a step back and then run, run, run around the landing until you Get There, urged roller-skating Risky Self, Jenny's impatient-opposite headstrong voice.

With a deep breath – nearly a sigh, but not quite – Jenny decided to be sensible. People somehow seemed to expect it, even if they hardly knew her, and Jenny had learned that if you do what people expect, they stay nicer for a lot longer. So, once again, her feet danced slowly – more slowly than she wanted – towards Where It Happens.

In and out of the bedrooms she went, peeking

but being careful not to poke. Her girl cousin's long pink fairytale room was behind the first door, with lots of odd curly paintings in it that were stuck onto a sparkly silver notice board with funny-shaped magnets. Next door, Jenny's boy cousin's bedroom was papered with posters and *posters* of the same football team dressed in red, with their redder-faced

manager always standing at one end, and wearing the same scruffy anorak to boot.

Hurry up, hurry up. It might have changed before you get there. Her Risky Self was getting restless, twirling her roller skates into bored circles in Jenny's head.

Be quii-et, hooted her Sensible Self calmly. *Only one rooom to go-o-o.*

Jenny carefully shut the door on the red posters and walked on.

Aunty Jasmine and Uncle Donal's bedroom was a lovely roomy room with shiny-knobbed brown furniture, a tall fabric headboard, splodgy curtains in the same material – and a rug that could never match *anything*. Aunty Jasmine had once told Jenny she *absolutely adored* that rug because Uncle Donal's mother had made it with her very own hands. But her eyes had gone up towards the sky and rolled around in her head while she said it. The rug was stripy yellow and blue and green and red and black, and reminded Jenny of tropical fish colours.

The Beginnings had almost ended. At last Jenny stood in front of the Best Bedroom of All.

The doorknob felt fizzy and hot in her hand. She turned it to the left.

The End Beginning

Thump, thumpity, *thump. THUMP!*

He's angry already, she thought. *He can* never *wait.*

The thumps were coming from an untidy heap of suitcases perched on top of the knotty wooden wardrobe. It was as if someone who couldn't be bothered to stand on a chair had flung them up there, one by one. They had lots of labels. Some of the bubbly letters had been filled in with friendly blue biro, others went straight up in strict black marker. Some of the labels were peeling off; others were still firmly stuck.

All the cases were proper rectangles and the faded brown of a bent-over lady's cardigan. Except for a small black hatbox that was jumping and jiggling like crazy.

Jenny stood just inside the door as the little round hatbox continued to buck and judder forward. It reminded her of the time Mum's car went wonky in the rain and a chatty man in a shiny yellow jacket came to fix it.

BANG! The hatbox hurtled to the floor.

Then, slowly – slowly – *faster* – *FASTEST* – the biggest suitcase of all toppled over beside it.

'Let me out. Let me out *this minute*!' The voice was muffled but the tone was not.

Jenny took three bold steps forward and undid the metal catches on either side of the hatbox lid.

A spindly arm punched the lid all the way off and the Gnome in the Hatbox sprang out.

The air whirled with stretching exercises as his skinny greeny-grey arms and legs pinged in all directions from his wiry body. His bulging eyes looked as if they might burst off his huge head.

'What took you so long?' he snarled, bouncing around on spread-out feet the size of tennis racquets.

Jenny knew from her other adventures that the grumpy gnome had a kind heart and didn't mean it. 'I got here as soon as I could,' she said, tossing her brown hair.

At this the cranky creature stopped his bouncing and glared at Jenny. Then he wheezed and hissed, slumping onto the large suitcase.

'Sorry I was ages,' said Jenny hastily, hoping to coax him into a better mood again. 'It must be really cramped in there. No wonder you're stiff and sore. Sorry.'

'My dear misguided girl, impressions are often

deceptive,' replied the Gnome in the Hatbox, quickly puffing up to his previous size and springing up again. 'This may look like your ordinary hatbox, but inside it's a red-bricked Georgian three-storey-over-basement packed with priceless antique furniture. And with panoramic views across the harbour ...'

He droned on, flapping his elastic-y arms to give himself flurries of satisfied pats on the back. Jenny sud-

denly felt tired. Mr Gnome's words were going fuzzy.

'And did I tell you about my car? It's a BHP31 twin-valve –'

Jenny just couldn't help it. She interrupted. 'Where am I going, Mr Gnome?' she asked, in her best fake-polite manner. 'Which one is my suitcase, please?'

The creature's delighted drone went putt-putt-putt and then stalled like a far-away lawnmower. His smirk faded.

'*Don't* call me Mr Gnome again.' He tossed his bald head and stuck out his rubbery lips.

'What, then?' Jenny felt confused. He had never minded being called that before.

'My name' – here the gnome stuck out his puny chest as if Jenny should be impressed – 'is Jeremiah.'

'Jerem– Jeremiah,' repeated Jenny carefully.

Jeremiah Gnome seemed satisfied with this. 'All right, then. It's time.' He heaved his oddly shaped body off the fallen suitcase and turned the case towards Jenny so the lock buttons faced her. The brown suitcase had metal corners to protect it, once silver but now rusted to a dark, dark brown.

'Off with you now and don't bother me for one second longer,' snapped Jeremiah. 'I'm very busy and important. You know what to do. Lid, if you don't mind.'

Jeremiah flip-flopped over to his hatbox and

turned to clamber back into it.

'No! Please!'

'What, *what* – for goodness' sake? Hurry up! My mushroom risotto is getting cold.' Jeremiah gave Jenny a slanty look. His eyes told her he knew precisely what she meant.

'How do I get back?' Sensible Jenny wasn't going anywhere without the gnome's instructions about her precious return ticket.

Jeremiah swivelled his fat head upon his fatter neck and puffed out his cheeks with a bursty noise that sounded incredibly rude. 'When you put your left foot first into the green shoes, you'll be back again. Now – *lid* – and be extremely fast about it!'

Jenny quickly pulled up the sleeves of her jumper and held out her left wrist. 'Will I be going back in history?'

Nodding, Jeremiah pressed a thin scaly finger upon the face of Jenny's wristwatch for a second or two. Her entire arm tingled for much longer than that.

'What do I have to bring back – are there souvenirs to collect? And what kind of people will I meet?'

By now the gnome was half inside his hatbox. 'My dear girl, I can't possibly divulge *those* details. That takes *all* the fun out of it.'

'Pleeeease, Jeremiah. At least tell me what I need to look for. *Pleeeease.*'

The Gnome in the Hatbox relented. Of all his trainee adventuresses, Jenny was by far his favourite. Although of course he'd never admit *that*. But he hadn't quite decided how everything was going to turn out – and he definitely couldn't admit that either.

'Antwerp and the North Pole were so easy-peasy,' he grumbled under his breath, disguising the complaint with phlegmy coughs. 'Oh well, I'll soon think of something clever for this escapade. I always do.' Jeremiah Gnome's belly rumbled as he cleared his throat.

'Oh, all right. You must find two souvenirs and bring them back to me. Green lights will guide you at every stage of your adventure. You must be extremely clever, though. It won't be easy. And now I'm off to have my delicious dinner, so don't ask me any more pesky questions, if you please.'

'But –'

With that the gnome flicked the back of a long warty hand at Jenny and warbled sarcastically, *'Adios, arrivederci, au revoir.'* And, with the fading of flat feet on stone steps, he was gone – for good or otherwise – back into his hatbox. Jenny bent to close the lid of the now-silent box and took a deep breath.

All she had to do was press a rusty button on each side of the ancient brown suitcase to make the locks flip up and the magic begin

Could she trust the bad-tempered gnome? What kind of green-light souvenirs was she looking for? What if she missed one of them? What if there *weren't* any green shoes? Or they didn't appear when she needed them? She might never get home to Mum and Dad again!

But the Gnome in the Hatbox had never let her down before. Hmmm.

Suddenly her Risky Self streaked up in Jenny's mind, did a showy stop-turn on her roller skates and took charge.

Get on with it, Jenny!

Click   right.
Left   click

The deep lid of the largest suitcase began to rise without Jenny touching it.

Step
left   and   in.

Step.   Right. In.

Eyes closed.   Whoooooosh!

Chapter One

Tock

Tick   Tock

Whirrrrr   Bongggg

(Pause.)   *Bonggggg*

Whirrrr   BONGGGGG

Tick   Tock

Tick

Before Jenny could open her eyes, her ringing ears knew she had arrived. But who would show her, this time? Jenny always liked to take note of where she was. (Mum called it getting her bearings.) Jenny stood up and gazed warily around, feet planted firmly in the middle of a golden platform. Her head was buzzing with all the whirring and bonging.

The high, high wall in front had all sizes and layers of jaggedy wheels rubbing against other

jaggedy wheels. Some went in the same direction, rolling a few notches back before winding forward again. Some did the opposite. Some got to click the whole way round. Some didn't.

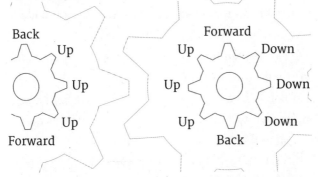

Back
Up
Up
Up
Forward

Forward
Up Down
Up Down
Up Down
Back

Jenny realised this was a fascinating thing to watch. But also that the rubbing and rolling and rising and falling were making her feel sick. Carefully turning her spinning head and her (thankfully) still-steady feet, she stopped staring at the high wheely wall to look around and up for her bearings. The other three sides of the tower were giant clock faces. A vast bell hung from the pointed bit above.

Jenny began to figure out the bits of inside-out numbers she could see around the bottoms of the clock faces. This would take her dizzy mind off the din, she decided. There was no rush. She checked the date on her watch. It was still today. *Hmmm.*

'Ahh – hahh – hahh – *hemmm.*' A hammy cough shoved its way through the ticks and tocks but was swiftly elbowed back in by the louder, constant sounds. Jenny's ears dug deep to find where from, but couldn't.

'Hello-o-o?' she called. Then, as the heartbeat in her head quietened a notch more, Jenny made a stronger attempt. 'Hell-O-O-*o-o-o*?'

Two golden half-circle doors popped open, bang in the bottom middle of the tick-tock wall. Inside, a spiky-haired boy dressed in a black leather jacket, snazzy white T-shirt and saggy blue jeans was doing casual pull-ups from the door jamb.

'Oh!' yelped Jenny. How had she not spotted that low, still space of the golden doors amongst the twirling and swirling?

'Hey dere, blud – yo is piff,' drawled the Boy in the Clock.

He dropped down onto the platform, swaggered forward and shoved his hands in his pockets.

'*What* did you say?' Jenny's voice pitched towards the roof bell in sheer surprise.

'Yo ma new co-dee!'

What is *he saying?* thought Jenny.

A couple of the words had been the same as in her language, but the others?

When the enchanted journeys began, the younger Jenny's dreamy ideal one used to be a golden-haired fairy godmother sweeping up on her satin padded broomstick and whisking her off to a sparkly palace for yummy fairy cakes (before bringing her all the way home again, of course).

But somehow it had never happened like that, and this latest adventure was starting to look dodgier by the second.

'I'm sick,' she snapped. Her insides were turning almost as fast as some of the clicking clock wheels and her head had begun to thump as well as spin.

'Yeah, yo is sick. Dat's what I tellin' ya. Yo is piff, like. Sick. *Ill.*'

Jenny began to perspire and tingle and feel cold all over her body, especially her forehead and the back of her neck.

Her thoughts began to race and rage. *Why have I come here? Jeremiah Gnome is* awful. *The boy's an* idiot. *I'm* never *going into another suitcase ever* again!

Green shoe.

Green shoe.

GREEN SHOE!

Biting her lip, Jenny stared at her new red trainers, willing them to suddenly match her green eyes. They didn't do anything whatsoever to help.

The bizarre, pale-faced boy was no good either: he wore black army boots and the scraggy laces weren't even tied up properly. A long defiant tongue poked out at each shin.

As Jenny raised her head, the Boy in the Clock gave her a hard stare. 'Chillax, blud. I is only stuntin'. Allow it. S'all piff.'

Jenny's Sensible Self chimed in. *Don't worryyyy. You will fiinnd the green shoooe when youuu are meant tooo. The boy is your friennnd.*

A shake of her head and Jenny's fears began to fade. She always had a guide. There was no-one else in this clanging golden clock except the boy – so it must be him and that was that. They would just have to find sentences that meant the same to both of them and get on with the adventure.

Jenny took a deep breath, shut her eyes and began counting. Everything would be fine. Her question-mark shapes would all be straightened out in good time, she told herself.

One-the-boy's-nice.

Two-I'm-quite-safe.

Three-the clock's great.

Four-need-more-time.

Four-and-a-half.

And-two-thirds.

Four-and-three-quarters.

Nearly ready.

Four-point-nine-nine.

Ready.

Four-point-nine-nine-

nine.

Five.

Right.

Stop.

Jenny lifted her chin again, feeling much better. The Boy in the Clock would help her explore. They would be friends.

He beamed brightly at her.

Then, unfortunately, all Jenny could think of to say was, 'Your nose is really *weird*!'

For it *was*. It had a rounded red bit at the tip like a toy light bulb. She was certain someone famous had the same nose, but couldn't quite remember who.

Jenny scrabbled around in her brain's question box

for a much kinder remark next. 'What age are you?' The instant she said it, Jenny felt self-conscious. Although she still figured it was better than nothing.

The boy stopped smiling in order to speak, but his blue eyes kept going. 'I don't really do time any more,' he replied slowly, the spikes in his hair flattening backwards as he spoke. 'It's stood still for me since I've been in this clock tower. I couldn't even guess at my age now.'

Whew! thought Jenny. *I can understand every word now. Brilliant.*

Although she did think it odd that a clock-boy didn't know his age.

'I'm Jenny. What's your name?'

'Ben. Benjamin Andrew Edward Pedro Arthur Philip George the Second, in the royal fullness of time.'

'Are you my guide?'

'Yes.'

'And do you live in this clock?'

'Yes. Didn't like the palace.'

'Why did you speak in that strange way before?' Jenny's head was so steady she hardly noticed the clock din any more.

'For fun. Come on, let's go.'

He nodded back towards the golden doors, open and waiting on the tick-tock wall.

'Hang on a moment,' said Jenny quickly, unwilling to move until she knew more. 'What's in there?'

'The globe-lift – to where the action is. And before you ask: yes, it's fast, but it's fine. There's even a gold-plated fire extinguisher. The health-and-safety department checked it ... oh – whenever.'

Jenny's contented nod stalled in mid-air at this last sentence. *Hmmm.*

'Are we invisible, like I've been before on other adventures?' she asked.

'That depends. And sometimes we can make wind. You'll need to remember that for later on, Jenny. It can drive them crazy but it's such fun.'

Ben's grin was crooked and wicked.

Jenny decided to save the rest of her question breath for later. She had a feeling she was going to need it.

'Step in and hold on,' instructed Ben, striding over and pushing both glistening doors fully open and back against the whirring clock wall. 'There's enough room. Just trust. Here we go.'

He entered the golden globe-lift and beckoned to Jenny. As she stood at the door, a rising roller-skate-y growl began to drown out the tick-tock hum.

Go away, Risky Self, she said firmly in her head. *I can do it myself. I don't need you.*

But thanks anyway, she added.

'Come *on*,' urged Ben. 'It's bong time again. They make your head fit to burst!'

A split second later, Jenny had stepped into the globe-lift and found her feet. Ben wrapped his hands around studded brackets beside one door and nodded to Jenny to do the opposite same.

Once she did, the Boy in the Clock began busily reshaping bits of his jet-black hair into spikes, using the shiny walls as a mirror. 'Pi-,' he muttered softly as he did so. 'Pi- Piff.'

He quickly gripped the studded brackets again as the globe's doors began to close. The glow inside dimmed to twilight as the drumming of time faded.

Down, down, down, down they inched, down to the clock tower's ankle, and then in soft slopey bounces towards its big toe beneath the ground.

As green light brighter and shinier than sunlight blazed into the globe-lift, Jenny looked quickly at Ben. He didn't stir. She could tell he was waiting.

Suddenly his wiry body crouched like a cat about to jump off a wall, making his arms stiff-straight and his knuckles white on the grips.

Jenny hastily did the same.

'Sick, *ill, PIFF!*' yelled Ben, the rest of his hair pinging up and out into stiff and stiffer spikes. (*That's what does it,* Jenny realised to herself. *When his hair's spiky, he does that weird piff-piffle talk. Hah!*) 'Three, *two –*'

'– ONNNNNNNNNE!'

26

Chapter One-and-a-half

The golden bubble plunged deep and deeper, going faster and faster before it slowed with a shudder and stopped with a tiny tilt.

'Open up, Ben.' Jenny was breathlessly ready for action. '*Hurry!*'

'Chillax, co-dee. No probs, like. Remote's in ma threads.'

Blast, thought Jenny. *I was right about the hair-spikes thing. Bad Blud Boy's back.*

Ben gave her a sharp look.

He kneeled to empty the front pockets of his jeans – the baggiest Jenny had ever seen – pulling out clump after clump of gadgets with all sorts of leads and plugs and blobby earphones dangling.

Shouts of 'Sick' and 'Ill' and 'Piff' each time he extracted something from the jumble said one thing, but the back of his neck getting red and redder told Jenny something quite different.

The four date squares on her watch were whirring so fast they were blurry.

Ben sat back on his heels, looking fed up. Then he jerked forward with a yelp, reached into a back pocket and produced the lost door remote control.

Whew, thought Jenny. *Let the adventure* begin.

Beep, beep, beep, beep.

'Doors'll take a mo, blud,' Ben told Jenny, bending to tie his laces. 'Cos we're in so deep, like. Oxygen's gotta get down.'

Jenny didn't like the sound of *that*.

While they waited, Ben popped on a set of earphones with tiny aerials sticking up from each side. Tapping his feet, he began a tuneless breathy 'Doof-doof-piff-piff'.

'Is there a spare door control, Ben?' asked Jenny sensibly, trying to quell her irritation.

Ben pointed with both forefingers up and over to his ears. 'Can't 'ear ya, co-dee,' he mouthed.

'A spare REMOTE *CONTROL*,' shouted Jenny. 'Or may I *KEEP* this one for YOU?'

Ben shook his head and chortled as he took out the earphones.

'What are all those gadgets for, Ben?'

'Piff stuff fo' later, like. Doof-doof-piff-piff. Yo'll see. Allow it, blud: doof-doof-piff-piff.'

With that, the doors swung open and slightly up. The light swirled out in a gentle corkscrew.

Jenny turned a full circle to get her bearings.

All was well. The damp tunnel ahead of them was well lit, although messy here and there in the distance with piles of leaves.

'Where *are* we, Ben?' asked Jenny. 'What's going to happen? Who will we meet?'

Ben chortled again. 'Not gonna tell ya what's up, blud. If yo need stuff as we go along, will do den. S'posed to be havin' an adventure, like. All about *not* knowin', co-dee. Chill-*ax*.'

Hmm, thought Jenny, after a long pause. She nodded her head. *Yes, he's probably right. I'd rather know more, but he's right.*

As Ben set off towards the green light-dot at the end of the tunnel, she thought he looked very pleased with himself indeed.

Chapter Two

'Goodly men and TRUE, search these *CELLARS!* Make HASTE, now – there's a deadly plot *AFOOT!* We must FINNNND-FIND those evil scoundrels *FORTHWITHHH-WITH-WITH!*'

The throaty voice boomed high and up and down and around in the echoing middle distance. Ben and Jenny were standing on a huge flagstone at the top of a flight of steps so worn down by centuries of mystery feet that they were much lower in the centre. The left-right left-right marching from all directions had become louder and much more together during the pair's brief trot along the tunnel from the golden globe-lift. Now each crisp stomp stood perfectly together in time and pace.

Abruptly the marchers' steps scattered, to be replaced by intense scratching (as giant mice might sound).

Jenny's heart flipped. She checked her watch. The date slots had finally stopped. 'One-six-oh-five,' she whispered. 'It's 1605.' Her heart flipped again, faster.

Ben bounded to the bottom of the stairs and

signalled to Jenny. A few moments later she was beside him. They were close to the action now.

'Are we invisible, Ben?'

'Wait 'n' see, blud.'

A short tunnel later and they had arrived.

Drip, *drip*-py, *drip*, plop, *PLOP*.

The noisily damp cellar beyond was dotted with barrels and lit solely by one square shaft of dull daylight from a high, high skylight.

Inside, a lean, dark-suited gentleman jumped around like a firework as odd droplets of water bounced off the wide wavy brim of his tall hat. He pumped the air with a large candle-shaped object in each fist. Black dust leaked from the candle-things, sprinkling and tinkling all around him, hanging in the air before drizzling into clumps upon the stony floor.

Jenny's heart began to thump-thump in earnest.

'Who *is* he, Ben?' she whispered, studying the strange man as best she could (which wasn't exactly easy, given that he was jiggling about so much).

Strands of dark-red hair and a matching thick beard brushed his old-fashioned white lace collar. Straggly eyebrows that met in the middle surprisingly made him look serious and thoughtful rather than scary or sinister.

He doesn't look evil enough to be one of the scoundrels that other man was shouting about, decided Jenny, *but I bet he has our first souvenir. I wonder what it is.*

Ben sniggered.

'Heaven preserve me from this confounded conundrum,' bawled the stranger, halting his odd dance with a shake of his head and darting his dark eyes just about everywhere.

His face glowed with a broad welcoming beam as he spotted Jenny and Ben peering into the drippy cellar. 'Now, little maid, strange lad, can *you* assist me?'

'Well, that answers *that* question, Ben,' muttered Jenny as they approached the smiling stranger. 'We're not invisible. But who *is* he?'

'Hey dere, big guy,' said the Boy in the Clock. 'How's it hangin'?'

'What sayest thou, sirrah? What rudeness is this, pray tell?'

Ben grinned. 'Not bein' rude, man. Just de way I talk, like. Chillax.'

'Well, be considerably clearer from now on – if you please. Harrrrummmph.'

'Good day to you, maiden.' The mystery man raised an arm to doff his hat to Jenny.

Pongggg-*gggg*!

One of the candle-thingies flew out of his hand, hit the ground with a wallop and whizzed around in circles before rocking to a full stop. There was a rotten-eggy odour and a rasping sound, like a match

being struck. A cloud of dust roared up.

Ben sneezed.

The man groaned. 'Oh, good youth, young lass, I believed, in a blinding flash of good fortune, that I had solved my –'

As he seemed upset (and the smell had thankfully scrambled off somewhere else), Jenny thought she had better say something kind as long as she had enough breath.

'You need some help, sir? With your *conundrum*?'

'Yes, yes. My conundrum.' The man cleared his throat twice and loudly, as befitted such a crucial problem.

'See here, I prithee. I am attempting to combust a goodly portion of firepower in this receptacle.' He stooped to pick up the now-empty candle-canister and wave it at Jenny and Ben. 'My purpose is to teach those dishonourable parliamentarians a lesson from the depths of the place where they make their ungodly laws. This, regardless of the sacrifice to my honourable self, I –'

The used-up candle-thing spluttered like a damp squib, puffed wispy smoke and finally gave up the ghost.

The confounded man crossly tossed it away and gingerly tucked its twin – still covered in rustling black dust and quivering every so often – into his coat pocket.

'What, you're trying to make a *bomb*? To blow up a *parliament*?' squeaked Jenny, horrified. 'Are … are you one of the … the *scoundrels*, then?'

'In truth I am,' replied the tall gent with a self-satisfied smile. 'But no-one will catch me and my dozen trusty henchmen! We *will* destroy parliament this very day! We *will* succeed!'

'Yay, man. Whadda guy!' yelled Ben.

Jenny's head was clanging with alarm bells of every shape and size you could possibly imagine. She vowed to find out more about whatever awful plot it was … but only when she got home to Mum and Dad. Because they weren't staying in this dangerous cellar for one – *second* – LONGER.

'Ben!' she scolded. 'Come on, let's go. He's trying to blow people up. Forget about whatever souvenir he might have. We're not going to help *him*!'

Mum would be furious if she knew I was talking to a bad egg like this, thought Jenny. *I'll ask Ben for the green shoes RIGHT NOW!* To her dismay, however, she realised that Ben and Scoundrel Man had struck up a lively conversation and there was absolutely no interrupting them.

Ben was waving his arms, his hair spikes practically sizzling at the tips. He resembled a skinny boy-sized sparkler firework. His new friend had begun a bizarre semi-dance, balancing a thick yellow piece of paper on one raised knee, scratching rapidly at it with a feather and nodding his head furiously.

It's a wonder his hat doesn't fall off, thought Jenny, as sourly as the earlier smell. *But I suppose his great big swelled head keeps it on.*

Ben was talking in such swift bursts she could only make out every-so-often words between all the 'piffs' and 'sicks' and 'stuntin's.

'Long matches … Gelignite … Nuclear fusion … Like … Laws of physics … Bucket of coal … Hairdryer … Like … Firelighters …'

As Scoundrel Man frantically scribbled Ben's new-fangled instructions about keeping his powder dry, Jenny glared from one to the other, hands on hips.

Scoundrel Man can't possibly understand what Ben is saying, she thought, close to blowing a fuse. *Half this stuff hasn't even been invented yet. They're a pair of idiots. And – we – really – must – leave – now. NOW!*

'Ben,' she cried. '*Ben!*'

The Boy in the Clock turned sheepishly back to Jenny. 'Sorry 'bout dat, co-dee. Got wound up, like. Dis guy is *well* sick wid all his stuntin'!'

Ben shook his new hero's hand so enthusiastically that the out-of-kilter pair nearly fell over.

Jenny's anger disappeared in a flash. *Scoundrel Man may be able to write all those bomb ingredients on his special paper,* she thought, *but he can't set anything alight in this damp dungeon. His wicked scheme will never work. Hah!*

Then she saw the light.

In slow motion a searing shaft of pure golden sunlight from way, way above was filling the square in the centre of the cellar.

Fizzzzzzle.

Hisss-SSSSS.

SIZZZZZZZLE!

The clusters of black dust on the ground began to hop and shiver as they dried and became live again.

'A-ha!' shouted Scoundrel Man, his eyes ablaze with relief, hope and – quite contrary to Jenny's first impression – wickedness.

He tugged the second canister back out of his pocket and hunkered down to scoop up fistfuls of gunpowder, trickling them carefully in at the top.

Sizzz-zzzzle.   *HISSSSSSS!*

'What are we going to *do*, Ben?' hissed Jenny. 'We have to stop him. We could all be *killed*!'

Ben looked reassuring, but his words weren't. 'S'yo adventure, co-dee. Yo gotta sort it, like. S'up to yo, blud.' Scoundrel Man gave a belly-deep grunt of satisfaction. His deadly weapon was full. He was ready to rocket.

'Now to magnify the sun's heat and ignite my *fuse*! With these barrels packed with gunpowder – boom! *Boom!* BOOM! Those rotten parliamentarians will be blasted to hell, where they belong. No-one defeats the mighty Guy Fawkes, KING OF *CONSPIRATORS*!'

Jenny listened for the rumble of roller skates. Nothing. No snappy Risky Self to tell her what to do. *Hmmm.*

Nor was Sensible Self's hooting anywhere to be heard in her head, either. It was up to her to stop deadly Guy Fawkes, so she'd better not blow it. Jenny shook back her hair and tried not to panic. She stared desperately at Ben for inspiration. He simply beamed and gave her an encouraging thumbs-up.

'It's all right for him,' she muttered. 'He's timeless!'

The wannabe bomber whipped out a beautiful golden spyglass and hunkered to harness the sun's harmful rays.

The short fuse on the stick of explosive began to crackle as the spyglass glowed and glowed – and became a bright, bright green! It *had* to be Jenny's first souvenir for Jeremiah!

Go, go, GO! For once, Risky Self and Sensible Self spoke with the same urgent voice.

Jenny launched forward and kicked Guy Fawkes on the nearest knee. He fell heavily sideways. The glowing green spyglass slithered out of his hand and across the cellar floor.

'Piff, co-dee, *SICK*!' whooped Ben.

'*Pleeeease* don't let it be broken,' implored Jenny as she scooped up the souvenir and they raced away from winded and groaning Guy Fawkes, towards the entrance tunnel and safety (for now).

'Oh, no! We can't get *out*, Ben.'

Excited men and boys in swingy red cloaks and fat black caps were flooding into the cellar, many of them ferrying sloppy buckets of water.

'SURROOOOUND HIM, MEN!'

Splash...   *Splash...*

SPLASH!

Hisssss-sss-SSSSSS...

'Dis way, blud,' hissed Ben himself, as he rapidly

41

steered Jenny towards a door at the back of the cellar and delved into a jeans pocket.

'Will your remote control open the door, Ben? Hurry. *Hurry!*'

'S'all right, co-dee. Gottit covered, like.'

Beep, beep, beep, beeeeeeeep.

The rusty iron door creaked outwards into another stony tunnel.

From the safety of there, they watched a sodden Guy Fawkes being manhandled into submission by many beefy yeomen and then marched left-right quick-smart left-right up and out of the dungeon.

Jenny gripped the (thankfully) intact spyglass even more tightly. '*Ow!*' Two raised pieces of metal were digging into her palm. 'Look, Ben – *look!* The letters F.D. – what do they mean? Is F.D. a person?'

Ben nodded as he held out his hand for the spyglass.

'Oh, I – I think I'll keep it myself. But thanks anyway, Ben.'

Don't worryyyy. It will be saaafe with himmm.

Despite her reluctance to hand over the souvenir, Jenny realised Sensible Self was only being practical. Her jeans pockets were too small to store the precious spyglass. She would just have to trust Ben to return it when the time came.

But who *was* F.D.? Jenny stared and stared

through the spyglass, hoping for an answer. And, sure enough, one by one these letters appeared and disappeared on its round glassy face.

A   F   A   M   O   U   S   E   X   P   L   O   R   E   R

Whole words came next.

H E L P   F . D .   G E T   T O

Just then Ben snatched the spyglass – and with a schlllll-ooo-OOOOP it was swallowed up into one of his bottomless back pockets.

'C'mon, co-dee. Too far to de next bit. We'll fly it, blud. Put yo left hand on ma right shoulder, like. Stuntin'.'

'But ... *but* ... *BEN*! I wanted to know where –?'

'Later, blud.' Ben put a finger to his lips and then a steadying arm around Jenny's shoulders.

They rose and moved silently upright through the muggy air along the passageway. As they flew, Jenny's annoyance vanished and her thoughts sparked back to Guy Fawkes. She had definitely heard about his gunpowder plot, but her head was spinning too much to remember the details.

For now, she had far more pressing matters on her mind – such as helping famous explorer F.D. to get to wherever it was, and whatever other magical mysteries were to follow.

Chapter
Three-and-rewind

A head scudded past and landed way, way down the wooden corridor Ben and Jenny had landed in after their upright flight. It paused before beginning a series of ugly, uneven bounces back towards them. Nose, crown, ear, cheek, forehead, ear – every single feature got a dull thwack on the floorboards as its wispy fair hair flicked in all directions.

Ben did a trippy-skip and spooned it up with his foot. Then he boinged it from knee to knee, rolling his own head as he did so.

'Yeuuuuuch,' shrieked Jenny. 'What are you *doing*? That's *disgusting*!'

'Keepy-uppy, blud,' he answered, grinning. 'Gotta get ma neck warmed up before headsies, like.'

'But it's a *head*!' protested Jenny.

'Chillax,' retorted Ben.

How I hate that stupid word, thought Jenny with a scowl.

'Chillax, chillax, chill*aaa*-aax,' taunted Ben, dunting his strange ball high in the air with an extra-hard knee-up. His neck was warmly ready for action now.

Duff, *duff*, duff.

Jenny felt before she saw the hands on her watch whizzing madly and the four date spots click-click-click-click forward to one-six-five-zero.

We've moved on forty-five years then, she thought. *It's 1650. Hmmm.*

The sounds of Ben and the head going head to head were turning Jenny's stomach much worse than the clanging clock in Chapter One.

And what happened next certainly didn't help.

A white horse streaked up with a 'naaa-aaa-eee-ay, naaa-aaa-eee-ay'.

Its ruffed, headless rider threw down his reins to swoop clumsily at Ben and his bizarre football. He fumbled with the head, shoved it crookedly onto his neck and scowled. Then he grabbed Ben, yanked him off the ground, threw the boy sideways in front of him and galloped off.

Jenny heard with horror the thundering hooves shrink to clicks along the long echoey corridor. Ben and the horseman were *gone*!

Her deep breaths were more like panicky gulps as she tried to form one of the counting question-mark-statement-thingies that helped her think more clearly.

One-where-is-Ben?

Two-*where-is-Ben?*

Three-WHERE-IS-BENNNN?!

Four-I-must-follow.

Five-I-must-FOLLOW.

Six-but-which-way?

Seven-*don't-know-where.*

Eight-make-a-plan.

Nine-what-to-dooooo?

Ten-NOT-A-CLUE!

Not

Aaaagghh

CLUE!

Well, that *wasn't much use. And I went to ten.* Jenny stood perfectly still to let her Sensible Self take over. Her cheeks puffed out with one last calming breath. She stared at the hairband-shaped cuts in the worn wooden floor, wishing and wishing for the hooves once more. *Please come back; please come back; please come back-back; please, back-back-back.*

For a moment she wasn't sure if it was in her head or in the air. But it was in the air. *Clack-clack-back-back; clack-clack-back-back.* And so on.

The horseback man had on such a straight face that Jenny didn't know if he was cross or pleased or neither of these or more than both. But she did know that she was very, very, *very* happy to see Ben again.

The Boy in the Clock gripped the saddle and slithered to the ground with a hardy thump.

As the horse's snorts quietened, Jenny sealed her lips and waited.

'Thy friend would have me return for thee, silent damsel.'

'Yeah. Couldn't leave ma co-dee.' Ben gazed at the ornate, painted ceiling, scuffed his boots and shoved his hands in his pockets.

Jenny was touched and relieved and glad at the same time. All she needed now was for someone to tell her what was *GOING ON*!

'Twelve long months I have lived in torture since that deadly day they had me beheaded,' boomed the angry horseman. 'It was treason, I tell you. *Treason*! Not mine – theirs.'

Go on, just ask him, Jenny. Her Risky Self was insistent (and actually pretty sensible as well).

'Those traitors escaped me but they will not do

so again! Revenge is mine. *Mine*. Miiiii–'

'Excuse me, please, but who exactly *are* you?'

Ben's shoulders heaved. Truly, Jenny was the funniest adventuress he'd had to date by several horses' heads and a very long nose.

'Come, come,' ordered the headstrong man, reaching for Ben and Jenny. 'We must not tarry. COME!'

'*No!*' shouted Jenny, stomping her foot so hard that the horse looked around and then did the same. 'We *won't.*'

Ben guffawed.

If he says that chillax word I – will – HIT – him, thought Jenny, ready to boil over.

Ben's spiky hair flattened with a squeak.

'Listen.' He spoke quickly. 'You signed up to the adventure – and as your guide I'm here to sort out stuff as we go along. Do you see *me* getting all worked up, Jenny?'

'No-o-o, but –'

'So what's your problem?'

'He's *headless*, Ben! What if it falls off and he can't see where he's going and then *we* fall off?'

Ben's gaze was steady, his voice gentle. 'If I make sure that doesn't happen, will you come on the adventure?'

'Yes.' Jenny's gaze was steady back as she sensibly stood her ground. 'As long as you'll make us invisible any time I say.

'Or,' she added quickly (just in case), 'the other way around if we need people to see us.'

Ben nodded solemnly. 'I promise, Jenny.'

At this the horse pawed the floor while its strange jockey muttered something about revenge tasting doubly sweet with two fine captives on board. (Thankfully Jenny didn't hear *that*.)

Ben put two fingers on her wristwatch, shut his eyes and made a catchy *haaaghh-mmmmmmmmm* sound in his throat.

'No go,' he said after a short silence with absolutely no clicks of Jenny's watch whatsoever.

Extracting a small-screened square gizmo from his saggy jeans, he began thumbing wildly at the buttons. Suddenly Jenny's arm was tingling right up to her elbow, as her watch clicked back eight times, to 1642.

The horseman's neck healed with a welcome squelch and his body became more solid-looking. Even the impatient white horse seemed far more content and stable.

Jenny worked it out straight away. *The horseman isn't a ghost any more,* she thought. *We've gone back in time to before he lost his head. That's much better.*

'Sussed now, co-dee. No probs, like. Sick, ill, piff! *Stuntin'*!' Ben had become his usual spiky-haired self again. 'Got yo back, blud. Allow it, like. Chill-'

'Thank you, Mr Horseman,' interrupted Jenny. 'We will accept your lift, after all.'

Ben hopped onto the horse first and then helped her up in front of him.

First they went windy fast, then bum-bumpity-bump slower with a quick breeze at lots of corners until they stopped in front of a grand Y-shaped staircase with 'LOWER HOUSE OF PARLIAMENT' written in swirly black metal in two lines along each side and slanting upwards.

'That was amazing,' whooped Jenny, untangling her hands from the bristly mane.

'Listen with great care, goodly pair,' ordered the nameless horseman.

Ben turned easily enough to obey, but Jenny had to do a weird sort of swively-lean. She was sorry she had. The man's eyes gleamed oddly and there was a thick layer of foam on his lips. His pointed, scraggy beard was soaked with sweat.

'The plan is thus,' he announced. 'I will storm this Lower House of Parliament and have those five traitors locked up in my tower by nightfall. I will drive them afore me through the streets at dawn on my trusty steed, Camilla, and they shall perish in public for their evil misdeeds.'

So that's the horse's name, thought Jenny. *I meant to ask it as well. I wish the horseman would say who he is now, though. I don't believe for a second he's going to kill five people in cold blood all by himself, no matter what he thinks they've done to him.*

'And I, King Charles George Pedro Hugo Oliver Klaus Arthur Henry the First, shall be hailed as the conqueror, the Mighty One, forever a regal hero in the true hearts of my loyal subjects.'

Hmmm. It will take a lot of breath to hail him. Jenny's neck was beginning to ache from swivelling back towards King Charles George Etc for so long.

'Onwards, in the name of JUSTICE,' he roared suddenly. 'ON-*WARDS*!'

Camilla reared, bucking Jenny against Ben and Ben against the infuriated king.

They rode to the top of the stairs and trotted along a long, long landing. At the very, very end, Camilla halted before imposing double doors carved with pigs, foxes, donkeys, weasels, wolves and goats.

King Charles Etc looked hesitant.

Then the brainy mare put her nose between the doorknobs, nuzzled at them gently until the left knob did a velvety click – whereupon she gave both doors a sharp horsey push.

The garbled shouting inside the parliament whooshed out like the hot air it was.

'The honourable gentleman's proposed bill would have neither rhyme nor REASON in law –'

Snarl ...   snarl ...   snarl ...

'Piffle, Dear Sir.'

'Piffle!'   'PIFF–*FLE*!'

... grunt, snort, wheeze, cough, sneeze, burp, shuffle, chortle ...

'– for the goodly people whom we strive to govern. I propose that we, the elected representatives of this great country, reject it *without* FURTHER *ADO*!'

Here, many 'Hear, *HEARS*' for the stout speaker in the middle of the chamber were almost drowned out by boos and hisses and bits of paper being clacked in the air like a flock of noisy geese.

After a few seconds of this, Jenny hadn't any quiet space left in her head to think anything new. Though she did say something from earlier (to do with the important promise Ben had made). 'Will you please make us invisible now, Ben?'

Beep, beeeeeep, beep, beep.

'Done, co-dee.' Ben squeezed the remote control back into his pocket. 'Invisible to all 'cept de king, blud. And whaddever yo is touchin', like, 'cept horses, gets invisible, too. Or ' – here Ben paused before meaningfully tapping the side of his weird nose (like a clumsy secret agent might do in a funny film) and winking at Jenny – '*whoever* yo is touchin', like.'

It was just in time. Green leather bench by green leather bench, the wigged, waving men saw King Etc and fell silent with nudges and grudges. Row by row, a hush blew through the wood-panelled parliament. It paused just short of silence.

They clopped further into the chamber.

'Ah-hem. Ah-*ha*-HEM,' blustered King Charles.

The hush grew louder.

Jenny was starting to feel sorry for the king. He had made such a fuss about revenge etc but now all those men were glaring at him with what looked very much like murder in their eyes.

'I SEEK FIVE TRAITORS TO THE CROWN.' King Charles the First had his second wind. 'THEY WILL NOT BETRAY ME A SECOND —' He paused to shoo Jenny and Ben off Camilla so he had more room to shout. They ran up the steps to the back of the stately terraced chamber and stalled at the end of an empty bench each. '— LONNNNGER. I MUST HAVE MY *REVENNNNNNGE*.'

With that the king unsheathed a jewelled sword, and, swinging it above his head, rode straight at the silenced speaker, a portly fellow standing slap-bang in the middle of the magnificent parliament.

The portly speaker ducked and, shaking his fists, stomped back to his seat.

'A-*HA*!' roared King Charles, jabbing the sword towards a guilty-looking gentleman sitting in the very front bench.

And then another.

'A-HA! A-HA-*HAAAAA*!'

'A-*HA*!'

Etc.

'He's found his traitor-men, anyway,' whispered Jenny. 'But Camilla can't possibly drive all five of them through the streets at dawn to their death. That's crazy. It'll never work.' Her out-loud wondering continued. 'He must have a better plan than that, Ben. All those snarly men are going to turn on him any minute now and he's totally outnumbered.'

'With all due respect, Your Majesty,' intoned a

skinny yet imposing parliamentarian from a small stone balcony overlooking the green benches of the Lower House of Parliament, 'you cannot interrupt these honourable proceedings and –'

'OH, YES, I *CAN*,' roared the king.

'Oh, no, you can't,' chorused the men in wigs, closing in from all directions.

King Charles tried to swing the sword again but

the portly speaker wrested it out of his hand.

'NO HARM MAY BEFALL ME, OH YE COMMITTERS OF *PERFIDIOUS TREASON!* FOR I HAVE TWO PRISONERS, TWO *HOSTAGES* TO ... to ... bargain ... with ...'

He stared around wildly but Ben and Jenny – invisible to everyone else in the stately chamber but King Charles – were far, far too many benches out of reach to be snatched as hostages. His eyes rolled in his head. Then he fell head first off Camilla and disappeared with a gloop into the babbling rabble!

His trusty steed reared and stomped into the air, but couldn't get near her beloved Charles. Squawking and screeching, the king's five traitor-politicians chased her backwards out of the chamber, to furious neighs and whinnies.

Jenny's heart sank. She didn't want to imagine what was happening to the king in the middle of all that. So she looked everywhere else until ... her eyes spied a polished wall cabinet just above the back benches on the other side and ... and ... saw that the edges of its glass doors were frosting a chilly bright *green*.

'Another *SOUVENIR!*' shouted Jenny. 'Let's go.'

Ben looked sly. 'Whadda bout de king, co-dee?'

For a split second, Jenny was torn. 'We'll get the souvenir first. Then we'll see.'

Grateful for her running shoes, Jenny raced down the parliament chamber, across and up again. She wrenched open the cabinet doors and scanned its contents.

A gold plaque inside proclaimed 'VERY IMPORTANT PEOPLE: SOUVENIRS'.

Jenny quickly spotted a white card with the initials F.D. in flowing green ink, followed by the stark accusation 'SPYGLASS: STOLEN'.

'Look, Ben. We're definitely on the right track,' she whooped. 'My second souvenir must be in here as well.'

The largest item by far in the cabinet was a wrinkly red leather book with 'A Voyage from Day to Knight, by W.R.' etched into the front cover.

As Jenny stared and stared, the faded gold letters began to turn green ... and then the whole book did the same.

This was it! The second souvenir for Jeremiah Gnome belonged to *another explorer*!

Grabbing the battered tome, Jenny opened it at random. The following shim-

mery words and letters appeared and disappeared across
a hand-drawn city map:

HELP   W. R.   GET   TO

And then, nothing else. Not another word, not
another letter.

Jenny turned to Ben, who was hovering nearby
and whistling low approval through his teeth.

The tumult around the fallen king below got
louder and louder as they sprinted back down the
steps with the magic souvenir.

'Off with his *HEAD*. Off with *his HEADDDDD*!'

'No-o-o,' yowled Jenny, thrusting the atlas
towards Ben and diving unseen into the crowd of
chanting politicians. She crawled in invisible zig-
zags until she reached the king's flapping head. 'You
mustn't hurt him. STOP!'

But of course only King Charles and Ben could see
or hear her, so Jenny's pleas also fell on deaf ears.

'*Pleeeease* be all right, Your Majesty,' she
entreated. '*Pleeeeeease!*'

'Burrghhh. Shlebbbbbeeeee. Mnnnnnnnahhhh,'
came the dribbling reply.

'Come *on*, Your Majesty,' implored Jenny, gently
shaking the king's shoulders. 'Please don't talk like
that. You're the *king*!'

At once the shouting ceased. There was an eerie silence as the parliamentarians backed off, leaving a ragged wide circle around Jenny and King Charles. They scratched their heads and noses in much wild-eyed confusion. Their jaws dropped.

'There is witchery afoot,' whispered the portly speaker, lowering the king's bejewelled sword in sheer disappointment. 'Where has he *gone*?'

'Egad – His Majesty hath entirely disappeared,' whispered back the skinny parliamentarian who had scolded the king from the balcony above and earlier. 'This is surely witchcraft at its most sinister.'

Of course! Jenny gratefully remembered Ben's heavy-handed hint. *As long as I keep hold of King Charles, he'll be invisible. Brilliant! We can escape!*

'Please get up, Your Majesty,' she wheedled, gently taking the monarch's arm as he shakily obeyed. 'This way. There, there. You're going to be all right now.'

But just as the pair had scuttled through and past the petrified politicians, the bewildered king twisted from Jenny's grasp!

'There HE *IS*! OVER *THERE*! THERE!'

Pandemonium reigned once more as the crowd rushed towards this new sighting of King Charles, the portly speaker gleefully brandishing the royal sword once more.

Ben grabbed the king and held the atlas over all three of them for protection – a split second before the portly speaker had a lucky strike. Rrrrrrrrriiiipppppp. The green died from the magic souvenir as the sword severed its flapping pages.

The disturbed mob fell silent again to gaze in confusion at maps all of a sudden fluttering around the chamber like curly cabbage leaves.

'You hang onto King Charles and keep him invisible, Ben,' yelled Jenny. 'I'll get the pages.'

Keeping the portly speaker – and his sharp sword – in her sights at all times, Jenny leaped and whirled and danced around the parliament chamber until she had gathered all the maps.

As the perplexed politicians saw the pages disappear in mid-air, they began fleeing the Lower House of Parliament, tearing at their wiry wigs and wailing.

Jenny finally returned to Ben and a dazed-looking King Charles, her arms full of crumpled pages. 'Whew! I think I've got them all now. *Whew*!'

Wheeeee-AWWWW. Wheeeee-*awwww*. Wheeeee-AWWWW.

Jenny was both alarmed and deafened. 'What's that awful siren, Ben? What's going on?'

Ben crammed the atlas maps and book cover into one of his back pockets with a glllllll-ooo-OOOOP and pulled out the square gizmo he'd used to click back eight years and banish Jenny's ghosts of earlier on.

It was blaring and vibrating like mad. 'Sorry, blud. Dead battery, like. In five, four, three ...'

Just then King Charles ran off again!

'Come *back*,' shouted Jenny.

Too late. The powerful screen had turned a blank, cruel green.

Chapter
Three-back-again

Clack-clack-back-*back*.   Clack-clack-*back*-*BACK*.
A familiar white horse, ears flattened and nostrils
flared, galloped up the wooden corridor once more
towards Ben and Jenny – but minus her rider this
time around.

She stalled in front of them, twitching and
shaking her head so hard that her lovely mane
fluffed upright.

'I'm really sorry, Camilla,' said Jenny softly,
checking the date before patting the upset mare.
'It's 1650 again and I don't think we *can* go back.'

She discreetly asked Ben with both her eyes and
her eyebrows.

'Nope, blud.'

'So where's King Charles now, Ben?'

Ben drew a finger across his neck with a serrated
'kkkkktchhh' noise. He began hopping from foot to
foot and rolling his neck like before.

As Camilla neighed in distress, Jenny mustered her best consoling tone. 'It's all right, Camilla. Wheeee. Wheee.'

'Whatcha doin', co-dee?'

'I'm blowing in her ear. I saw it in a film. Horses like it.'

After several whistly blows, Jenny was sure Camilla's chocolatey-brown eyes looked less sad.

'So-o-o,' she deduced, 'King Charles stormed parliament in 1642 – and that nasty lot put him in prison for years and then beheaded him?'

Ben nodded. 'C'mon. Put yo foot in my hand, blud. Up yo get.'

Jenny stayed put. 'And now he's a ghost, but Camilla isn't – because she escaped the politicians' clutches?'

Ben gave Jenny a dramatic double thumbs-up.

'Let's find him, then.' She vaulted gracefully onto Camilla's back.

The forlorn horse did several left-rights left-rights off the corridor before stopping at a studded wooden door and nodding her head at it, slowly and wisely.

Jenny pushed and pushed, but it wouldn't budge. 'Blast,' she wheezed. 'It's locked. Ben, can you use the remote control again?'

'No power, blud. Gotta recharge, like.'

Jenny ran back a few steps and charged at the door.

Crreeeeeeakkkkkkk.

Whoooooooooshhhhh!

Squeeeeeeelchhh-thud-d.

'Owwwww!'

She had bumped into King Charles in the open doorway, knocked his head clean off and stumbled into a dusty old library!

'Sorry, Your Majesty. I was only trying to rescue you,' explained Jenny, quickly getting to her feet.

King Charles the First appeared moved by this declaration. Following Jenny back into the room, he scooped up his head and wiped its teary eyes with a floppy white handkerchief.

'But why did you lock yourself *IN*?' Jenny was nearly speechless.

With that the ghostly king slumped to the floor, head in his hands. Its eyes were rimmed red.

'I dismissed those devious parliamentarians many times so I could rule alone. My ways were *BEST, I tell you. BEST!* But they paid five dastardly lawyers within their ranks to sign a decree and declare me *MAD*, and seven years later they beheaded me! Me, their mighty monarch' – his voice broke – 'accused of *high TREASON!*'

'King Charles, would you mind putting on your head, please?' asked Jenny firmly. She was finding it difficult to listen because she didn't know where to look.

Squelch. Creak-twist-creeeeeak. A smaller, final squelch.

Whew!

'Thank you.'

'And behold what the demon blackguards who roam these hallways do to me. Ayee – it is too much to bear – they rub salt in my wounds with their dastardly feet when they consort in regiments of eleven. That is why I must hide from them thus.'

'What's he talking about, Ben?' whispered Jenny, staring hopefully at her guide's hair – which helpfully went flat so he could explain.

'The other ghosts steal his head for football matches, Jenny. Remember when it bounced up to us at the very beginning of this adventure? He's been headless for a full year and they haven't given him a minute's peace.'

'That's *awful*.' Jenny had to blink back tears.

'What will you do now, King Charles?'

The monarch shakily rose to his feet after pulling himself, mostly, together. 'I must surrender to my foes,' he replied wearily.

'Oh, please don't give up, King Charles,' urged Jenny. 'There must be *something* you can do to keep your head?'

But the beheaded king merely sobbed in reply.

'*Pleeeeease* don't be this miserable for all eternity,' she begged him. 'You've got your lovely Camilla to keep you company, after all. Perhaps if you talked to the other ghosts they might find a different football and leave you alone?'

'You speak the truth, kindly maid,' said the king with a rueful smile, gradually cheering up. 'I shall try forthwith.'

Poor King Charles's plight seemed horribly unfair to Jenny. It was a terrible punishment for entering parliament unannounced – even on horseback. Jenny promised herself she would learn more about what had happened to him, after she got home.

As Ben slipped through the open door that launched them into the next part of their adventure, Jenny paused for one last glimpse of King Charles the First, and was delighted to see him murmuring happily into clever Camilla's ear as his beloved mare whinnied contentedly back.

Chapter Four

Boom! *BANG!* BOOOOMMMMMMM!

Heart pounding, Jenny peeped around the edge of the adventure door. She could see the bottom parts of huge patched sails billowing in the breeze and a worn wooden deck speckled with water. It all smelled very fishy indeed. *I'm definitely on a very old ship,* she thought. *But where on earth is Ben?*

'Psssst! Quick, co-dee.'

Almost before Jenny could take it all in, Ben appeared in front of her, bundled her through the doorway and hoisted her up and over the edge of a small rowing boat sitting high and dry upon the galleon's ancient deck.

Wow, this looks exciting! thought Jenny, peering around for her bearings from inside the much smaller boat. (And, as an afterthought: *Gosh, Ben's far stronger than he looks.)*

'Sick hiding spot, like,' crowed her quick-thinking guide. 'Well piff.'

A hook-nosed man clad in tight brown breeches,

black thigh-high boots and a lacy cream blouse strode under the ship's sails, firing orders in all directions. From her vantage point Jenny could see that some of his crew were lighting fuses on cannons jutting from the hull. Others filled cannonballs with gunpowder from huge hessian sacks, while more others poured more gunpowder into smaller, saggier sacks.

BANG!   BOOMMMMM!

'Missed *again*!' roared Hook Nose. 'You are *FOOLS*! FOOLS! The Spanish are in our sights and we must STRIKE THEM *DOWN!*'

By now Jenny's watch had rewound to 1581. *Hmmm.*

Could Hook Nose be F.D.? Jenny wondered. *Or W.R.? They were explorers, so they must also have been sailors. Did they fight the Spanish, though?*

Hook Nose began roaring anew and scratching frantically at rough brown bristle on his cheeks. 'Where is that infernal *SPYGLASS*? We are LATE for HER *MAJESTY*. We must MAKE HASTE to the *DOCKS*! We dare not miss our target *AGAIN!*'

He strode to another rowing boat directly behind Ben and Jenny's hideout one and began tugging at it. 'Over *HERE*!'

Four muscly henchmen rushed to join him.

'One – and – two – and – three – and heeeee-EEEEEAVE,' they chanted, dropping the rowing boat overboard.

'Load her up, men,' commanded their skipper.

Thud. Thud-DY. *Thud*. Thud-dety-THUD.

Seven small but deadly sacks thudded into the small rowing boat.

'Serious stuntin' comin' up, co-dee. Yo gotta see dis.'

Hook Nose began to scratch even harder and faster at his bristly face. His crew cowered and covered their ears as Ben and Jenny looked on.

Rrrrr-aaaa-SSSPP. Long sparks flew from the captain's stubble as he grabbed a long wooden pole, ignited it and hurled it, flaming, down into the rowing boat.

Sizzling with explosive intent, the small boat immediately shot off towards two sailing ships bearing down fast upon the galleon.

BOOOOOOO-MMMMMMM-*MMMMMMMM*.

'Gadzooks,' roared Hook Nose. 'They are DESTROYED! Only one left!'

Whooooo-sshhhhhh.

Jenny watched awestruck as the third and final Spanish sailing ship hurtled towards them against a smoky sky, fuelled by the explosion – and wedged alongside their galleon!

Within moments the sailors from it had swarmed

73

onto the galleon's deck, where swashbuckling fisticuffs erupted between the two sides.

Slap. Thump. *Smack*. Thwack. And so on. Etc. And more.

'Where's Hook Nose gone?' whispered Jenny.

'Aaa-rrrr-*ggg-HHHHH*,' bellowed the skipper, running back up on deck to fell enemies right, left and centre with a jagged cutlass.

Soon there was only one Spaniard left on his feet and the commotion had ebbed entirely.

'El Draque – ze Eeenglish dragon man,' sneered the last man standing as he squared up to Hook Nose, fists poised like a boxer's. 'Ee makes ze hot *fuego* with heees face.'

As the fiery captain touched the tip of his weapon to the Spaniard's chest, Jenny held her breath.

Pleeeeease don't kill him, she beseeched.

But the captain's henchmen simply hauled the defiant captive across to his own ship, followed by a crooked line of whimpering and limping Spaniards.

'PLUN-*DER* it,' roared Hook Nose, following in their wake.

'What's going *on*, Ben?' said Jenny, standing up to survey the deserted galleon. 'He's the ship's captain, that's for sure. But is he W.R. or F.D.?'

Ben shook his head. 'Not gonna tell yo, blud. More fun dis way, like. Sick. *Piff!*'

Jenny dampened down her rising temper. 'Have it your own way. I'll probably figure it out by myself, anyway. Should we explore this ship, then? Now that they've all gone over to the other one?'

Scrambling from the rowing boat, Ben turned to give Jenny a helping hand.

As she hit the deck, a brainwave struck. Jenny spied a line of water buckets, and she threw a bucketful of water over Ben!

'*Now* tell me,' she yelled triumphantly. 'I know you have to explain things properly when your hair spikes are flat! *Hah*!'

Ben bent double with laughter as he wiped his sopping hair. But as soon as he could speak, he explained. 'It's 1581, and we're on the *Golden Hind*, the galleon of explorer Francis Drake: the F.D. on your spyglass. He's being knighted by the queen, but the Spanish Armada skirmishes have made him late. She's on her way to the docks now, for the official dubbing ceremony on board his ship.'

'Thanks, Ben. That makes sense now.'

'You're welcome, Jenny,' answered Ben, tugging a towel from one of his huge pockets and starting to dry himself. 'But did you have to use *that* water bucket? I stink of rotten fish! Ugh!'

Ben rubbed so vigorously at his hair that a cloud of steam formed around his head.

'And do we use the magic spyglass to help him get to the docks more quickly, then?'

'Bit o' stuntin', blud. Piff stuntin', like.'

Jenny sighed. Ben's hair was spiky again. *At least I've discovered lots to go on with,* she thought.

Biff. *Biff.* Dunk. *DUNK!*

Ben raced to look over the galleon's starboard side, with Jenny close behind.

A man was climbing up a rope ladder onto their galleon, the *Golden Hind*! His scarlet sunburned face clashed with his greasy auburn hair. His clothes were filthy and full of holes.

'Help me!' he hissed, pointing back down to a small sailboat that was thudding and listing against the *Golden Hind*. '*Zounds!* I must save my prized discoveries afore they are *lost FOREVER.*'

'So we're not invisible, Ben?' whispered Jenny. 'I didn't get a chance to ask before your hair dried.'

Ben shook his head.

'Do we need to be?'

Ditto.

With that the raggedy man jumped back into the thudding boat – which was sinking fast – to lift a half-full sack of potatoes up towards Ben. 'Bring this on board, goodly lad. My treasures must live on. The great Walter Raleigh's explorations to brave new worlds must not have been in vain.'

'Walter Raleigh,' mouthed Jenny. 'He's the W.R. on the atlas! So they're *both* here now!'

Ben had barely heaved the sack of spuds over the guardrail when Walter Raleigh hurled a metal box marked 'Tobacco' after it and climbed nimbly aboard the *Golden Hind*.

'You must help me find a safe harbour for my spoils,' he panted, staring jerkily around. 'They must remain out of sight or that pirate Drake –' he spat over a grubby shoulder '– will surely claim them as his own!'

'What about the small rowing boat we hid in earlier?' suggested Jenny.

Walter Raleigh's sun-glazed eyes looked her up and down inquisitively. Then he smiled warmly enough and nodded.

'C'mon, bluds.'

Soon Raleigh's prized potatoes and tobacco, plus the explorer himself, were all concealed in the rowing boat.

Ben and Jenny were just about to climb in after him, when:

Clatter,   CLANG,   *bang*,   clunk,   *WALLOP!*

The crew of the *Golden Hind* were back in eager numbers from their plundering expedition on the Spanish ship, dragging bulging treasure chests between them. Their captain strolled on board after his delighted men, with layers upon layers of jewelled gold chains looped around his neck.

'Quick, co-dee. Over here till de coast's clear.'

As the triumphant sailors disappeared below decks, Ben and Jenny sidled forward to the prow of the *Golden Hind*.

Schlllll-ooo-*OOOOP*.

Wordlessly Ben gave the golden spyglass to Jenny as they huddled at the very front of the ship.

'I can see land, Ben!'

But as the vessel began to race full steam ahead, the spyglass began to glow and glow – until it turned an angry, hot red in Jenny's hand.

'What's going on? Why is it doing that?'

Ben took Jenny's wrist and pointed the spyglass slightly to the right. Immediately the shaft cooled and returned to golden.

A series of green numbers appeared on the glass.

'I bet it's telling us the fastest way,' marvelled Jenny.

Ben whistled approvingly, staring intently at the numbers as he swiped his hair flat.

'Ten DEGREES to the *STARBOARD*,' he boomed suddenly.

Two or three bellowing echoes up the line and the galleon was on course.

Soon they were slewing up a wide river with a

bustling city on both banks. Crewmen dashed around, lashing ropes and dropping an enormous rusty anchor over the stern. As the galleon shuddered to a stop at the busy docks, two of them held a gangplank ready to slide across onto dry land.

Ben and Jenny crept closer and hid behind a heap of sailcloth. Trumpets blared as the queen approached for the knighting ceremony.

She flounced on board with a chattering entourage behind. Her red hair was drawn tight and bizarrely far back off her forehead. Her puffy dress and stiff tiara were dotted with pearls and rubies, as was a massive ruff at her neck.

Captain Francis Drake had donned a frilly black cape which matched his lacy blouse but was totally at odds with his stern expression, hooked nose and crimson-veined bristled cheeks.

'What treasures await Her Majesty, sir?' enquired the sovereign. Her tone was quiet but her eyes glittered mercilessly. 'We trust our royal faith in thee hath reaped deserved rewards and we can knight thee accordingly?'

'Oh, yes, Your Majesty,' replied Drake smugly, bowing and scraping and flouncing so enthusiastically that his cape swung out like a skirt.

'Then let us marvel at your brave trove, Sir. *FORTHWITH*!'

'C'mon, blud.' Ben held out a sheet of black sailcloth to Jenny. He wrapped himself top to toe in another length of it, like a makeshift cloak, and quickly melted into the frayed edges of the crowd.

Clutching the spyglass tightly to her chest, Jenny held her dodgy disguise together with her free hand and gingerly followed suit.

She needn't have worried about being visible. In many hot and stuffy cabins below, the royal hangers-

on were far too busy sniffing fragrant barrels filled with exotic spices to notice stowaways in makeshift sail-cloaks.

'Oooooooohhhhh.'

'Aaaaa-hhhhhhh.'

'MmmmMMMMMMmmm.'

And the riches purloined from the Spanish Armada delighted them even further.

'Gnnnnnrrrrrrrrgh.'

'Nyeaaaaa-wheeee.'

'Splurrr-TTTT-*TTT*.'

The ecstatic entourage streamed back on deck, led by Her Majesty. Head thrown back, she cackled and joyfully punched the air.

Ben and Jenny hung around at the back. Then, as Drake and a companion approached with low voices, they ducked behind a thick coil of rope just in case.

'Forsooth, thou art a skilled navigator, my second-in-command,' Drake murmured to the other man. 'My gratitude is heartfelt, sir, for thy timely instruction to change course on the starboard and bring us here with such speed.'

'But − *but* − I *didn't* change course,' spluttered the

explorer's right-hand man. 'I thought *YOU* had ...?

Ben grinned knowingly. 'Sick. *Ill.* Givvus de spyglass, blud.'

Jenny readily held out the enchanted souvenir – but it slipped from her hot hand and skidded along the deck to land ... right at the feet of Francis Drake!

The explorer's eyes lit up. 'My lost glass!'

Jenny knew she shouldn't, but she did anyway.

'Excuse me, Mr Drake, sir,' she said, rising from behind the skein of rope. 'I know this spyglass belongs to you, but ... well ... I need it, please. It's a souvenir from my adventure, you see.'

Already regretting the impulse that had driven her to show herself, Jenny was especially conscious of her shoddy sail-cloak.

'Egad! Didst *thou* navigate us hither with it, maiden?'

'Erm, yes, sir. Well, sort of. May I have it back, please?'

Francis Drake shook his curls emphatically and gave a scornful harrumph as he tucked the spyglass into a high boot.

Jenny's heart sank. Her face fell. *The cranky gnome is going to be* so *annoyed,* she thought. *I really need that F.D. souvenir.*

Seeing Jenny's obvious upset, Drake softened. 'I cannot give it to thee, maiden, for it is shortly to be a gift for Her Majesty. But, if I may, I shall present thee with this token instead.' Drawing from his cloak a miniature galleon with 'Golden Hind' painted on the bow, he stepped forward and offered it to Jenny.

'Thank you, sir,' she replied, feeling better (and braver) already.

As Jenny discreetly put the tiny ship into her jeans pocket, she steeled herself to snatch the spyglass. Except that, the very moment she tried, Francis

Drake turned to stride towards the excited gaggle of people surrounding the queen. Jenny's swiping hand came back empty, her stopgap cloak fell wide open and she couldn't help giving a loud gasp!

The explorer turned back. His eyes hardened and narrowed when he saw Jenny's jumper and jeans. Then he stepped forward again – and menacingly this time.

Jenny began to panic.

Ben jumped out from behind the skein of rope and, with a firm hand on her back, steered Jenny towards the gangplank.

As ripples lapped at the side of the real, full-sized *Golden Hind*, he shoved her off the sailing ship – and the water below began to swirl, bubble and turn green.

Chapter
Four-and-more

Jenny scrabbled-swam towards a rusty iron ring on the harbour wall but the choppy waves kept sweeping her just out of reach.

'GRAB my *HANDS*.' In a trice Ben had hauled her out of the water.

They crouched on the dockside, shivering and soaking. A gale howled and whistled and moaned around them.

Jenny could barely hear herself think. She looked down at her dripping watch with a horrified squeak.

'It says 1585, Ben,' she shrieked. 'Four years later than when we were on the *Golden Hind*. Is that RIGHT?'

Ben nodded.

Despite having to screech, Jenny knew she had to ask as much as possible while Ben's hair was plastered to his head, for that was the time he made most sense.

'Are we going to meet Walter *RALEIGH* again now? And use the atlas to *help* him?'

Ben nodded, closing his eyes as huge raindrops pelted onto his face. 'He's being knighted as well, but he doesn't know the WAY,' he bellowed back. 'He's always getting LOST! He needs the ATLAS so he can be *KNIGHTED*.'

'By the same queen?'

A third nod. 'Queen B–'

Suddenly the storm stopped. Masts tinkled gently on cargo ships. Stevedores began loading and unloading crates, shouting good-humoured orders to each other. Gulls wheeled against a clear blue sky. If there had been bluebirds, they would definitely have tweeted.

'Piff, co-dee,' said Ben.

Blast, thought Jenny. *How does he do it? He's completely dry again in no time, and talking his usual piff nonsense stuff. And I'm still soaked.*

'Ben, will you make me dry as well, please?'

Beep, beep, beeeeep, beep.

'*Thanks*, Ben!'

As Jenny turned in the direction of a low huddle of dockers' cottages, Ben nudged her back towards the line of anchored ships and pointed to the biggest and nearest galleon.

'Look, blud. Dere, like.'

A perfectly groomed Walter Raleigh was jogging down the gangplank, sweeping his arms outwards and up as if he was the lead actor in an extremely dramatic play.

'I wonder will he recognise us?' mused Jenny, as the explorer approached. 'It's been four years.'

Ben grinned, because, with even more flowery gestures, Raleigh brushed past them as if they absolutely weren't there.

'Oh!' said Jenny. 'We must be invisible again, Ben. Are we?'

Ben nodded. 'C'mon, co-dee.'

They followed the explorer through the cobbled streets while his strange rehearsal continued.

'I'   'wondered'   'lovely …
A-hem.
'I'   'wondered'   'LOVELY'   'as'   'a' …
Ah-HAH-hem.
'I'   'wondered'   *'LOVELY'*   'as'   'a'   *'CLOWN.'*

'He's got it all *wrong*,' hissed Jenny, extremely and quickly annoyed. 'We learned that poem at school. He hasn't got a *clue*!'

Smirking, Ben pointed to Jenny's watch.

She waggled her fingers as she counted dates, back and forward.

'Oh, I see,' she said with a giggle. 'That poet won't be born for centuries.'

'Sick. Piff, like. *Stuntin'*.'

'Ayyyy-eee*EEE*,' moaned Raleigh, halting abruptly.

He looked around in confusion.

'I cannot for the life of me memorise my fine verse for Her Majesty. Moreover thus, I must locate where her carriage awaits me or I am *doomed*.'

Glllllll-ooo-OOOOP.

Ben presented the atlas – slightly sticky but at least back in one piece – to Jenny with a bow.

'How will he see it, Ben?' she wondered, before remembering that if they weren't touching the magic book, it could be seen.

THUD!

Raleigh turned at the surprise noise and scooped the battered red atlas off the ground in delight, to pore over its pages. 'My maps! My wonderful city maps! Hurrah!'

In quickening twilight he jogged confidently this way and that, through narrow uneven alleyways and along in front of haphazard rows of thin and thick houses. Jenny and Ben skipped along behind.

Finally the explorer reached a grassy square with arched stables full of horse-drawn carriages along one side. Unerringly Raleigh made for the grandest one, which was studded with gems like giant stuck-on sweets and had a complicated golden crown embossed on each side.

'Giddy-UPPP! Post-HASTE! Don't spare the *HORSES*!' bawled Raleigh to the coachman as he threw the atlas through an open window and leapt in after it.

Ben nimbly grabbed a twirly handle, hopped up on the outside shelf of the carriage and pulled Jenny up beside him in one smooth movement (as if he had done this many times before).

'This is *brilliant*,' she shouted, as they sped off through the rest of the city.

Jenny looked inside the coach to see Raleigh putting on a huge conical collar. Then he painstakingly combed his beard.

'Oh, Ben,' she giggled. 'He looks like a dog being treated for fleas!'

Before too many more twists and turns they clopped to a halt in front of a stately creamy-grey building with lots of columns and fluttering flags.

Night had fallen.

As Raleigh sprinted up the steps with Jenny in hot pursuit, he stumbled and dropped the magic atlas.

'Get it, Ben,' she yelled.

Ben seized the souvenir with a smile (and pocketed it with a familiar gllllll-ooo-*OOOOP*) just as the explorer turned – and saw exactly nothing.

'Where hast it gone?' panted Raleigh. 'Drat and darn it – I must present myself to Her Majesty forthwith. I have no time to search for my precious book.'

He sprinted into the magnificent hallway and then down the furthest corridor off it, his enormous collar wobbling inelegantly.

Stopping at a set of double doors, Raleigh wiped his brow and face with a huge handkerchief before turning the glittering green knobs.

'Looks like he's just in time,' whispered Jenny, as they followed Raleigh into the plushest of plush ballrooms. 'Thanks to *us*!'

The deep carpet and flocked wallpaper were such a blaze of scarlet that Jenny had to close her eyes for an instant because this grand place definitely wasn't easy on them.

A bewigged footman was presenting a heavy sword to Queen B–

'What's her name, Ben? You never did finish.' Jenny didn't expect an answer, but it was worth a try.

Silence.

'Oh, well. I'll just have to call her that, then. Queen Bee.'

Ben chortled.

A shuffly queue of elderly gentlemen had formed in front of the monarch. She raised the sword and tipped the first in line on each shoulder. Before being knighted, each man offered a present to the queen – who nodded at a nearby row of bored ladies-in-waiting to take it away.

Jenny and Ben sat cross-legged in front of the crowd of good-humoured onlookers.

One of the almost-knights held out a quacking duck to Queen Bee, who looked horrified. 'Arise, Sir Mansion of Duck Ponds,' she gulped, nodding to the line of waiting ladies.

The plumpest lady-in-waiting scooped up the bewildered duck and waddled off, muttering something about nipping to the palace kitchens for the rest of the evening.

A giant bottle of red wine from another almost-knight squeezed a broad smile from Her Majesty.

'Arise, Sir Merlot of Fine Wines.'

Instead of kneeling, however, Walter Raleigh struck an exaggerated pose when it came to his turn.

'My gift is my verse, Your Majesty. This one's for you,' he proclaimed.

A-HEMMMMMM.   'I'   *'wondered...'*

Her Majesty looked daggers as she held the sword impatiently over Raleigh's head.

Oh, no, thought Jenny. *He needs a better present*

than his awful poem to please the queen. I wonder if I should...

Glllllll-ooo-OOOOP.

'Stuntin',' said Ben, producing the atlas again with a flourish.

Jenny really didn't want to surrender her Raleigh souvenir, but, on the other hand, it was clear that the explorer was making Queen Bee very angry. And nobody wanted *that*. She would just have to explain it to Jeremiah when she got that far. So Jenny gently placed 'A Voyage from Day to Knight, by W.R.' at the feet of the disgruntled monarch.

Kneeling at last, the explorer looked dumb-founded to see it appear – but then gratefully proffered this vastly better gift.

Queen Bee grumbled for a moment, then nodded.

'Arise, Sir Walter.'

As he heaved himself up, three misshapen objects fell from Raleigh's breeches and hit Jenny on the head.

'What on earth ...?'

Ben held down his hair spikes in order to break into delighted doggerel. 'One potato, two potato, three potato ...'

'Oh, come *on*, Ben! I can't possibly bring *these* back to Jeremiah.'

But Jenny quickly saw the funny side – and, as it

probably was almost time to get the green shoes and go home, she scooped up the cheeky spuds to bring to Jeremiah Gnome. They were better than nothing, after all. And Sir Walter Raleigh *had* brought the first potatoes to Europe, she knew that much. So they weren't just any old souvenirs.

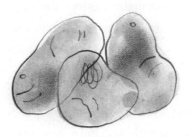

The moment Jenny touched the potatoes, the air around her turned a misty green and began to whirr and whizz and shudder.

The Beginning End

Seated on her padded purple throne, a present-tense queen chewed the end of her pen and scowled. She was trying to solve a crossword in a newspaper that was tightly yet untidily folded more times than you'd think possible. Her silver curls and grey gown shimmered as much as each other. The gems in her tall, bulgy crown blinked and winked.

'Schnaw-*whooo*. Schnaw-*WHOOOO*!'

The puzzled queen took a breather from her crossword. She bent forward to give equal numbers of pats to two jowly overlapping dogs snoring in a basket at her feet.

'Ooo's Mummy's best girls, then. Mummy's best *GIRLS*!'

Jenny gazed even more around for her bearings. She and Ben were standing at the back of a high, panelled parliament hall similar to, but even grander than, the Lower House of Parliament King Charles had stormed centuries earlier. Its empty leather benches were red instead of green and the soaring

golden doors beside Ben and Jenny were cleverly carved with owls, eagles, stallions and stags rather than the donkeys and goats etc of before. Like the Lower House of Parliament, this Upper one had burnished-wood display cabinets dotted around the walls. Jenny's watch had fizzed forward to practically today's date.

'Are the green shoes here, Ben? And are we still invisible?' she whispered.

'Gotta see for yerself, blud.' Ben folded his arms so suddenly his leather jacket squeaked. He looked as if he was in a very bad mood indeed.

Just then the queen flung the newspaper onto the vacant throne beside her with a pained sigh and rubbed at her forehead. Her wrinkly visage had become greyer than her dress and Jenny was reminded of when poor headache-y Mum had to lie in a darkened room for the whole afternoon.

Squeeeeeze, squuuuuuuueeeeeeze, went the queen's fingers on her aching forehead.

A bubble stretched from her lips, flipped free and floated off, followed by three more. Pop! Pop! Pop! And words formed in them, one by one.

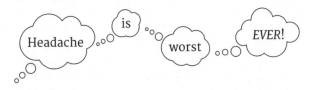

Jenny's mouth was a great big O as she christened the queen Migraine Lady.

'Why is she doing that thing with the bubbles, Ben?'

The new frowning Ben had begun to tiptoe away – but he didn't get far. The queen's bubbly thoughts flew over and squeaked and scrubbed at his hair spikes until they lay down in defeat. Ben dove and wove and dodged, but, although two bubbles went pop, the other two did not. There was no escaping the truth at this point.

Jenny burst out laughing, for once. 'Now your hair's flat, Ben, you *have* to answer my question.'

'The queen can never complain out loud, even to herself.' Crossly, Ben began tugging at his hair to get it into its normal rebel style. 'So that's what she does instead. Satisfied?'

Jenny was (for now).

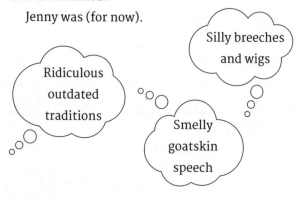

The miserable monarch was in full flow, huffing and puffing bubbles.

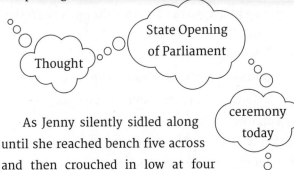

As Jenny silently sidled along until she reached bench five across and then crouched in low at four down, the bottom half of Migraine Lady's gown began to glow green.

I bet she's wearing my magic shoes, whooped Jenny in her thoughts (although as quietly as possible for whooping). *But how will I see for sure? And how will I get them from her? I really need to know whether we're invisible, but Ben's gone all cross and won't tell me. Hmmm.*

Scree-ee-CH! Roller-skating Risky Self plonked herself back into Jenny's mind. *Run up to her, fast as you can, waving your arms. If she reacts, you'll know you're visible.*

And if she doesn't, thought Jenny, *then I'm not. Good plan!*

No-o. Make a test souuunnd first and then seee. If she can hearrr you, she can seee you tooo. This second suggestion from Sensible Self sounded far wiser to Jenny, so she decided to risk that instead.

Jenny beckoned to Ben, who was one row further down, to join her. He did so, but dragging his feet – and with another deep scowl.

'Whooooo-OOOOOO-ooooo,' she went.

'Seriously, blud?' he snapped. 'You're acting like a *ghost*, like?'

Jenny nodded her head defiantly (wondering what on earth was wrong with Ben, and hoping he'd be back to his usual sunny self before too long).

The queen's head stayed totally still.

Zig-zagging to seat number three across, Jenny whirled her arms and 'whoooooooo-ed' louder and longer, but all that happened was that Migraine Lady's laments blew bigger and sadder. Her mournful eyes stared straight at and through (clearly invisible) Jenny.

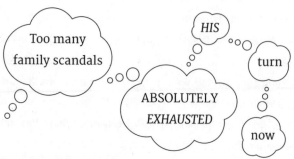

Right, thought Jenny.
The queen definitely can't see or hear us.

Now she was sure, Jenny strolled up to the throne platform, kicking up bubbles.

One of the snoozing mutts raised its head and looked lively for a moment. Jenny held her breath. Letting sleeping dogs lie here might be tricky. Fortunately the dog merely gave a gigantic slobber and fell into another deep slumber.

Whew!

Jenny skipped up to tired Migraine Lady and carefully squished between the thrones. Her cheek felt hot against the mottled marble tiles as she tried to peek under the hem of the queen's gown. But the dress sat tight to the floor in stubborn heavy folds and wouldn't budge.

Jenny looked at bad-tempered Ben with the absolute best please-help-me expression she could manage. 'What am I going to do, Ben? How will I see?'

Faced with Jenny's pleading gaze, the cloud over Ben mostly cleared. He smiled a weaker-than-usual smile. Then he helpfully did a breathy gadgety 'doof-doof-piff-piff', bowed low in front of Her Majesty and began puffing hard at her dress.

Jenny remembered immediately. *If I can make wind like Ben said way back on the golden clock platform,* she thought delightedly, *I can blow at the hem of the queen's dress and see her shoes. Hah!*

Jenny's first two puffs were too weak, but the

third one rewarded her with a rustle of satin and – a sparkle of green. Jenny's stomach fluttered with anticipation. She had found the shoes! Going home would be her next step.

As Jenny stood up to consider how to get the magic green shoes, Migraine Lady shivered and flung back her head to emit a fresh set of complaint thought-bubbles.

Then she returned to her crossword, tutting, but looking a lot less pale.

'Apologies, Your Maj. So sorry, dearest wife!'

The late man rushed in, the colour of beetroot. He flopped so hard onto his throne that the rows of medals on his dark-green soldier's uniform flipped and jangled.

Jenny was transfixed. *His nose! It's exactly the same as Ben's.*

'Ben – *look!*'

But Ben was already studying Nose Man intently, his blue eyes glistening.

'Are you all right, Ben?' asked Jenny. 'What's going on?'

'Sick, blud. Ill, like. *Chillax.* Piff, co-dee. Stuntin', like. *CHILL-AX!*' Instead of being cross, Ben now seemed dazed and disconnected

Oh, dear, thought Jenny. *He's losing the plot.*

She waved a hand in front of his blank eyes. 'Ben, listen to me. *Listen!* Can you make them see us? I need to get the queen's shoes, so I have to be visible.'

'Erm – nope, blud. Chillax. Chillllll-*aaa-AAXX*.'

'No, you *promised*, Ben,' replied Jenny firmly. 'A few centuries ago, agreed. But a promise is a promise, no matter when.'

Ben noisily folded his arms again and sulked.

'What's the matter?' asked Jenny gently. 'Is it that soldier? The queen's husband? Don't you want him to see you?'

'Don't belong, like. Tried it. Didn't like it, like. S'all a loada stuntin'. C'mon, blud. Tower's best for de likes of me, like. *C'mon!*'

Jenny felt really sorry for Ben, but she had a problem of her own to solve. 'Isn't it your job to guide me?' she wheedled. 'I need to get *home*. Maybe you can make *me* visible but not you?'

But Ben wasn't budging. 'No can do, co-dee. S'all or nuttin', like. Dem's de rules, blud.'

Jenny realised she'd have to get the Boy in the Clock to co-operate – and quickly too. It really was time for her to go back. 'Will you tell me about why you live in the clock tower and not in the palace, Ben? Maybe I can help?'

It was a long story, but, holding his hair down flat so he could, Ben told it concisely and well. About how his empty-headed brothers and sisters were always letting the side down with their silly pranks and about how his regal parents (yes, Migraine Lady and Nose Man) were frequently away on foreign trips meeting other kings and queens, which meant he got the blame for the awful behaviour of the younger royals. In the end, thoroughly fed up, he had fled to the clock tower for a bit of peace and quiet.

'But time stood still for me there and I lost track of the years,' he said wearily. 'I thought they'd ask me to come back to the palace straight away – and they didn't.'

'Oh, Ben,' replied Jenny sadly. 'I'm so sorry it's been like that. But perhaps if they see you again they'll ask you? Maybe they didn't know where you'd gone?'

At first Ben looked doubtful. Then a hopeful smile glimmered.

Gradually he began glooping gizmos and gadgets from his never-ending pockets, discarding them with a 'Nope, no juice' or a 'Dead, like' – until one final sizzling lead snaked through his fingers.

'*Sick*,' said Ben in an oddly high-pitched voice, nervously steering Jenny up towards the thrones and wrapping the live wire around their combined shoulders.

Pooooouuuffffff!

Hiiiii-*SSSSSSSS!*

Jenny knew it had worked, because Nose Man sniffed sharply when he saw Ben. Migraine Lady stifled a sob. 'It *is* him,' she gulped, almost under her breath. 'But he looks so *young*.' Then she gasped. 'Of *course*. He's been in the clock tower.' With that, the queen shuffled her newspaper many unnecessary times and glared at Jenny.

'Yes, girl? Who are *you*? Why have you appeared here like this? What do you want?'

With a wobbly curtsey, Jenny racked her brains for something to say that would make the grouchy queen surrender her footwear.

'Erm – well, Your Majesty – I need you to … to give me your *shoes*.'

'Harrummmphhh.' Nose Man placed a golden monocle over his left eye and peered at Ben.

The monocle reminded Jenny of her prized spyglass. *Now, there's a thought! If I still had it … maybe I could use it to bargain with and go back?*

Yooouuu doo have it. Yoouu got it from Guyy Faawwkes aafterr- rrr Fraancis Draake toook it baaack.

So I did, thought Jenny. *Even though Guy Fawkes was earlier in my adventure, it was later in time. Thank you, Sensible Self. This could come in really useful.*

'Ben?' she whispered. 'Have you still got the spyglass, please? Remember you took it from me after I kicked Guy Fawkes to get it?'

With a familiar schlllll-ooo-OOOOP from a ginormous gloopy pocket, Ben silently produced the precious souvenir once more and handed it over.

Jenny held up the spyglass and watched Migraine Lady's eyes widen like saucers. She wanted that spyglass, Jenny could tell. But would she exchange the shoes for it?

Ben and Nose Man continued to size each other up like wary bloodhounds not sure whether to pick a fight.

The queen scratched her forehead and looked puzzled for a moment, still staring intently at the spyglass. Then she rose and, with Jenny close behind, rushed over to swing open the doors of the nearest display case. Jenny immediately recognised the plaque inside: VERY

IMPORTANT PEOPLE: SOUVENIRS. It was the very same cabinet that had been in the Lower House of Parliament all those years ago.

The W.R. atlas looked even more battered, and someone had typed a different note about F.D.'s exhibit, in ANGRY CAPITALS:

SPYGLASS: STOLEN –
GENEROUS REWARD
OFFERED FOR SAFE RETURN.

Brilliant! thought Jenny. *That's it!* She waved the spyglass under the queen's nose and pointed to the words 'GENEROUS REWARD'. Then she pointed down at the queen's feet.

'I need your shoes, Your Majesty,' she said steadily.

The queen sighed, but then nodded and took the spyglass from Jenny. She placed it delicately into the cabinet and scrunched up the note.

'Fetch my wellington boots, m'dear,' she commanded her soldier husband, striding back to her comfy throne and sinking into it.

He immediately halted his extreme staring match with Ben, clicked his heels and began stiffly marching out of the magnificent chamber.

Jenny began to tingle all over at the thought of

seeing Mum and Dad again – although it had been an incredible adventure and she would really, *really* miss the Boy in the Clock.

Who was now standing in front of his own mother, head cocked to one side, looking expectant and defiant at the same time.

I wonder if Migraine Lady will fix it. Pleeese ask Ben to live at the palace. Pleeeeease, beseeched Jenny in her head.

At that the queen beamed a wonderfully kind and regal beam. She took off her winking crown and held it out to Ben.

'Put it on,' she said. 'It's yours. We knew you'd come out of exile one day. We searched and searched but we couldn't find you. Welcome back. It's about time.'

Ben stood shock-still.

'Go on, Ben,' urged Jenny. 'Take it. You know you want to.'

For once, Ben hadn't a smart reply – but as he accepted the crown without a word, Jenny detected the hint of a smirk. He sauntered over to the nearest bench and carefully placed the priceless jewelled headgear on the shiny red leather.

'Sorry, Your Maj. Sincere apologies. Couldn't find the wellies at first, m'dear.' Nose Man's returning face was tomato-coloured.

Her Royal Majesty pulled from each welly-boot a long wonky sock in as many blinding colours as

Aunty Jasmine's beloved (or not) bedroom rug and put them both on.

'It's all solved, dear,' trilled the queen. 'We're certain-sure it is. *Solved!*'

It was as if a great weight had been lifted from her weary shoulders. 'He's coming back to the palace. Isn't it *wonderful*?'

Nose Man twitched. For a split second he showed his crooked yellow teeth in a delighted grin. Then he went 'Haarrrrrumpppph' again – and lifted his wife's rustly newspaper so high that no-one could see his face.

The now-mellow monarch presented the magic green shoes to a grateful Jenny.

'One needs to walk the dogs by the duck pond anyway, dear, so one's wellies are *much* better for that. Here you are. *Bon voyage!*'

She bent to rouse the lazy dogs with more coochie-coo baby talk.

'Oh, Ben – thank you *very* much. I'll never forget you,' vowed Jenny, hugging her guide. 'So, are you going to live with your family now? You really should.'

The Boy in the Clock gave a secretive smile as his hair spikes flattened. 'Time will tell.' Then he grinned. 'By the way, it's a rounded rectangle.'

'*Pardon?*'

'The shape you didn't know upstairs in Jasmine's

house.' Ben nodded towards the dogs' basket, outlined its shape with a forefinger and then cut off the corners with four gentle wiggles. 'A rounded rectangle.'

Jenny's mouth became a perfect circle. *How on earth ...?* But she knew better than to expect an answer.

She sat on the bench beside the blinking crown to put on the green shoes.

In the next breath she was catapulted (almost) home from a huge golden building with spires and turrets and complicated sticking-out bits on all sides – and a striking illuminated clock tower high against the starry purple sky.

The Middle End

The second before Jenny opened her eyes she heard a 'slurpy-slurp-SLURRRRP' and what sounded a lot like Jeremiah Gnome's voice happily murmuring 'yum-yum-YUMMMM'.

The Gnome in the Hatbox was seated at one end of a long mirror-smooth dining table in a huge room with display cabinets crammed together along one wall. Jenny was at the other.

'Mushroom risotto – my favourite,' he trilled, spooning up the last morsel of his much-anticipated dinner. 'Delicious!'

At once Jenny had to pinch her nose. What a stench! She cleared her throat. 'Ah-ha-hemm.'

'Yesh, yesh, you're back. I see you,' said the Gnome in the Hatbox, flapping a spindly green arm behind his back to dispel the windy smell. 'Sho, how was your adventure?'

He topped up his goblet of wine from a giant bottle labelled 'Merlot – by Royal Appointment to Her Majesty', took a sizeable gulp, and then hiccupped several times in quick succession.

'Ooops,' he giggled.

He shuffled over to sink into a padded purple armchair beside the crackling fire and began gingerly rubbing his warty pot belly.

'It was fantastic,' enthused Jenny, once the pong had gone (and she'd got over her irritation at the gnome being, quite clearly, a bit tipsy). 'I met lots of interesting people from history – although I need to learn a lot more about them now.'

'And how was your guide?'

'He was called Ben, the Boy in the Clock – and he was *brilliant*! I wasn't sure about him at the start – he spoke so strangely. I was worried he wouldn't be reliable. But he totally *was*!'

The Gnome in the Hatbox sniggered as he lit a fat cigar from a metal box with a picture of Sir Walter Raleigh on top. He glanced sneakily sideways at Jenny. 'So, where are my souvenirs?'

'We-e-e-e-lllllll ... The thing is, Jeremiah, I did get them, honestly. But then I had to give them up in order to get back. I do have things to prove I met the two explorers, but – well – I don't think you'll want them.'

'Hand them over, quick-smart.'

Jenny thought for a long moment, then reluctantly stuck her hand into her jeans. Whatever about the silly spuds, she really wanted to hang onto the tiny *Golden Hind*. But then again, she couldn't have her magical adventures without keeping Jeremiah in the best possible mood.

'Yeuchhhhhh!'

The combined goo of rotten potatoes and a disintegrated model galleon made a sticky mess in her hand.

Jenny looked so disappointed that Jeremiah relented. Tossing over a thick flowery napkin so she could clean her hands, he asked: 'Is thish what you're looking for?'

She got up and followed his greeny-grey finger towards one of the display cases.

It had a gleaming gold plaque in the shape of a rounded rectangle along the top, engraved with the words 'J.S. – VERY IMPORTANT ADVENTURESS'.

On the glass shelves were displayed souvenirs from all around the world – including a familiar miniature wooden sailing ship and an ornamental sack of golden potatoes.

'Those are my initials,' marvelled Jenny. 'And my souvenirs! Wow! How did you make that happen?' Her left hand began to tingle again. 'What else will be going in there, Jeremiah?'

'That's for you to discover next time, my dear.'

'Oh, I can hardly wait for my next adventure!'

'One last loose end.' The gnome pointed to Jenny's sparkly green pumps.

Jenny clapped both hands over her mouth. 'Ooops!' Mum would be extremely surprised to see her wearing those instead of the red running shoes they'd bought just last week.

'I'll change them jush as you finish the last leg,' said Jeremiah. 'Now step your right foot forward and close your eyes.'

In a trice Jenny was magicked back into the Best Bedroom of All with a blaze of go-green and – poouuuu-ffff! – just as she appeared in the open brown suitcase which had brought her to everywhere this time, her footwear turned to stop-red.

Until the next time.

The Very End

Bongggg! Bongggggg! BONGGGG!

Jenny sat up so suddenly as the television news began striking the hour that her glass of water spilled onto the sofa.

'Not to worry, Jenny, pet,' said Mum, dabbing quickly at the thick red cushion. 'It's getting very late, though. You can sit with us for two more minutes, but that's all.'

'You were very quiet on the way home from Jasmine's and hardly said a word at dinner,' added Dad. 'Mum and I were worried about you. Are you feeling all right?'

Jenny smiled in her usual open, friendly way.

Mum looked pleased and relieved, clicking off the volume button to talk to her daughter, who had such a vivid imagination. 'Did you enjoy Aunty Jasmine's, Jenny? You were in your favourite room for ages.'

'Yes, I had an *amazing* adventure!' The words tumbled out. 'I met a boy in a clock who watched over me *all the time* and a man who had an *evil bomb*

117

plot and a horseman who *lost his head*!'

Pride slowed her voice for this next part. 'And I helped two *explorers!* They were all famous people who made history happen, Mum. They were called –'

'Now, dear, it's time for bed. Off you go.' It wasn't like Jenny's mother to interrupt but Jenny was getting far too excited.

Dad grinned reassuringly. 'Don't worry, Jenny. We'll research those people properly tomorrow after school, I promise.'

Jenny went hot, then cold. There was a picture of a golden spyglass behind the serious man reading the news! And the words 'MYSTERY REAPPEARANCE' were scrolling across the bottom of the screen!

Jenny wriggled forward for a better look. A huge golden clock came next.

'Mum, can you turn on the sound, please?' she squeaked.

Ben was in front of the clock on the television, seated in a jewelled carriage. He looked older and more mature somehow, but it was definitely Ben. He was wearing the tall crown and waving enthusiastically at crowds of silently cheering people.

'Mum! *Please!*'

'Sorry, darling. The remote control must be here somewhere. I had it a moment ago.'

Jenny launched herself towards the television, but

it was too late. The newsreader was already beaming goodbye. Cracks of wonderful fireworks made the pointed clock tower look even more golden-brilliant against the flashing colours of the night sky. It was incredibly beautiful, as all happy endings are.

Jenny glanced at her watch. The small diamond where the two steady hands met winked with the purest of green lights – just for a split second.

MYSTERY REAPPEARANCE

The History Bit

If you haven't already guessed, the city featured in this story is London, the wonderful capital of England and the United Kingdom. I took my inspiration from several ancient English traditions (although they didn't all get to be in the book):

Parliamentary Practices

Ever since Guy Fawkes's failed gunpowder plot in 1605, Yeomen of the Guard search the Houses of Parliament cellars before the reigning monarch arrives for the State Opening of Parliament. The State Opening takes place in the House of Lords (the red benches) as the ruling king or queen hasn't been allowed into the House of Commons (the green benches) since Charles I stormed it in 1642. In turn, MPs (who sit in the House of Commons) cannot fully enter the House of Lords for the State Opening or any other event – they must stand behind a railing.

Knightly Knowledge

Towards the end of each year, men are knighted and women become dames at Buckingham Palace, the official London home of the UK monarch. In bygone days it was only military heroes (and men) but nowadays the honour rewards sterling work of all kinds – and the recipients were never obliged to give the king or queen a gift in return. The person kneels on a stool in front of the monarch, who lays a sword blade on their right and then left shoulder (dubbing). Contrary to popular belief, the sovereign doesn't then say, 'Arise, Sir/Dame ...'

Although I've tweaked facts and figures to make the book more fun, the historical characters Jenny meets in *A Clock or a Crown?* really did exist:

Guy Fawkes

(Probably born on 13 April 1570 and definitely hanged on 31 January 1606) was part of a twelve-man plot to blow up King James I at the State Opening of Parliament on 5 November 1605. The ringleader was Robert Catesby and it was Guy Fawkes's job to guard the explosives.

PS: Fawkes posed as a servant to source the gunpowder – the plotters had thirty-six barrels of it in their rented cellar below the Houses of Parliament.

Charles I

(Born on 19 November 1600 and beheaded on 30 January 1649) believed he had the divine right to make up his own laws. However, the politicians didn't agree and tensions mounted until Charles I's failed bid in 1642 to arrest five of them in the House of Commons and charge them with high treason.

PS: I made up Camilla – sorry – but think she's brilliant and am certain Charles would have too.

Sir Francis Drake

(Born circa 1540 and died on 27 January 1596) was only the second person to navigate around the world, from 1577 to 1580. Queen Elizabeth I (Good Queen Bess) came to Deptford in south-east London on 1 April 1581 to reward him with a knighthood on the *Golden Hind*.

PS: Historians believe that a French nobleman called Monsieur de Marchaumont actually carried out the dubbing.

Sir Walter Raleigh

(Born between 1552 and 1554 and died on 28 October 1618) was – among many other things – a poet as well as an explorer. Like Francis Drake, he fought the Spanish Armada and sailed to America. His claims to fame include bringing potatoes and tobacco back to the UK. He was a favourite of Queen Elizabeth I, who knighted him in 1585.

PS: His poems are excellent, if you like that kind of thing!

Thank you for reading *A Clock or a Crown?* And maybe we'll meet again in another Suitcases adventure.

Caroline Logue
April 2015

The Thank-you Poem

To the Folks in The Big House, who nourished with care
the strangers who came to be made more aware.

To her who e-bargained and created some space
and the publishing team who saw the right pace.

To Aer Lingus, bold Michael and airlines galore,
and the agents of nations who helped me explore.

To those on the bus who threw me your words:
drunkards and phoners and gigglers and nerds.

To pedants and pol corrs and workers away
with a glaze on their face at the end of the day.

To the teacher who listens, and listens some more,
to the waves on the beach from that place at the door.

To those who believe, leaving talent aside –
when you work from your guts there is no place to hide.

To all those who wonder, you know who you are ...
may the dreams in your eyes let you travel afar.